Fall Rush

A Southern College Novella

By Meda White

Fall Rush
Copyright © 2014 Meda White

Editor: Andrea Grimm
Cover Artist: Kari Ayasha, Cover to Cover Designs

This is a work of fiction. Names, characters, places and occurrences are a produce of the author's imagination. Any resemblance to actual persons, living or dead, places or occurrences, is purely coincidental.

ISBN: 1941287026
ISBN-13: 978-1-941287-02-6

DEDICATION

To My Sisters—whose humor and tenacity never cease
to inspire and amaze. Much love to you both.

ACKNOWLEDGMENTS

Thank you to my critique partners, Ali Hubbard and Christina Kirby. May we all enjoy many years of publishing success and sharing the stories of our hearts.

Chapter One

Embry Harris rushed in the door, late for her first real day of work. She tried to catch her breath while she apologized to the manager and tied an apron around her waist. She'd been through training and had shadowed a few experienced servers, but she was still nervous about waiting tables by herself. It seemed so simple when she watched others do it, but balancing a tray of food and drinks was no easy feat. The owner of the sports bar had taken a chance on her, and she didn't want to let him down.

It was so unfair she had to work for spending money her senior year of college. If only her parents would've let her transfer to another college closer to home, things would've been better financially and otherwise. They'd insisted she stick it out at the main campus for her last year. She'd offered to quit the sorority to cut back on expenses, but her mom had nearly had a conniption fit.

Embry was a legacy and her grandmother, mom, and both of her older sisters were sisters in the Greek sense of the word. Not only was she forbidden to quit, she was forced to live in the house, spending even more money her parents didn't have.

As the youngest of three girls, Embry was grateful there was any money left for her college expenses. Her parents had dipped into her education fund to pay for her sister's lavish wedding. Since Omni was marrying into money, they'd wanted to impress the groom's family. If only they'd had a simple beach wedding like her eldest sister Indi had had two years earlier, life would be easier. The truth was Indi's marriage to Cobie had changed Embry's life, and not in a good way.

If Embry could survive this year and graduate, she'd move far away from South Carolina and never look back, which was funny considering her naivety when she'd started college three years earlier. Her goals then were to get a degree and fall in love with a fraternity boy who would propose at graduation. That stupid little girl was long gone.

She shook those thoughts off as she filled her drink order and lifted the tray, careful not to tip it too far in any direction. She practically held her breath as she made her way to deliver the beverages. She set them down without dumping them on anyone.

The lady with mile-high hair sipped her soda. "This tastes like diet."

"Yes, ma'am, that's what you ordered."

"I changed my mind." She shuddered. "I

thought you heard me."

"Okay, regular Coke. I'll be right back."

"And I need lemon for my tea." The balding man tapped his glass.

"I need a straw." The kid swung his head to get his too long bangs out of his eyes.

Embry reached in her pocket and pulled out straws for everyone.

"I'll be right back with Coke and lemon." Embry smiled and strode away.

"Miss, can you get our waitress? We're ready to order," a lady called as she passed.

It was one of Embry's tables, so she stopped to take drink orders on her way to the other errand. It was a mistake because they ordered drinks, appetizers, and food, which overwhelmed Embry to the point she forgot the first table until they stopped her again.

She spent most of her shift apologizing to people, but never so profusely as when she knocked over an ice water into a man's lap while she was clearing away dishes. Pete, the owner, wasn't going to be in until later, and the manager eyed her like a hawk spying a field mouse, ready to pounce when she least expected. After cleaning up the mess, she checked on her tables before going to the newest table in her section. She'd rather sit in a fire ant bed than go to that table, but they were customers too.

She put on her biggest, fakest smile and approached. "Can I get you guys something to drink?"

"Tease-me-Embry, what are you doing working here? Being a tease wasn't paying the bills?"

"Just earning some spending money. What are you drinking, Chase?" He was the guy she tried to date her sophomore year. When they'd gotten hot and heavy, she'd panicked and run out on him. He started calling her that name when she'd been too embarrassed to return his calls afterward.

The table of fraternity brothers placed their orders, each giving his own little dig in turn. She'd only frozen up on Chase, but to hear them tell it, she did it to every brother on campus. She'd stopped trying to date or have sex after that. Of course, they stopped asking her out too. Being a pariah was hell on a sorority girl's love life.

* * *

Stede Bennett held the door open for his GiGi. She'd been asking him to take her to the place he worked. He would've done it just for the asking, but he had another motive. His boss, Pete, wanted him to check out the newest hire, a sorority girl. Stede had taken a few days off to work on a school project, so he hadn't met her yet.

He held the chair out for GiGi. Of all the people he'd missed while away serving his country, she'd been the one he'd missed the most. She was the fun grandmother, the one who kept him after school and on weekends while his single mom worked three jobs.

GiGi had been a domestic engineer most of her life, until his grandfather passed and she'd had to find a way to support herself. She loved being a sorority house mother, and Stede was pretty sure she was born for the job. She was spry for a grandmother, and she'd taught him how to treat a lady. A few of his fellow Marines used to give him hell about his gentleman-like behavior, but he had the last laugh when the ladies asked him for a ride home. It worked, almost every time.

"Can I get y'all something to drink?" A pretty little brunette pushed some loose hair behind her ear before she poised her pen to take their order.

"Embry, how's your first day?"

"Oh, GiGi." The girl hugged his GiGi hard and started to tear up. "I don't think I can do this."

"Now, now." GiGi patted her back. "It'll get easier. Stede, honey, give me your handkerchief."

Stede was already reaching for it, so he handed it to the girl who straightened and used it to blot her eyes.

"I'm sorry." She looked over her shoulder. "My boss is staring." She blotted once more and gave it back to him.

Stede started to correct her on the boss comment, but didn't want to give himself away yet. He'd already let GiGi know they were on a reconnaissance mission.

"Embry, this is my grandson, Stede, the Marine. Embry is one of my girls." GiGi patted her girl's hand.

That meant she wouldn't be an objective observer.

"GiGi, we agreed not to tell your girls we're related," Stede said out of one side of his mouth.

She put her hand on her chest. "Oh, I forgot. Embry, you can keep a secret, can't you?"

"Yes, ma'am."

He wasn't sure how they were going to get out of this mess. As a bartender, Stede didn't want the sorority girls to know who he was because they might ask for favors, like free drinks. He couldn't afford to buy the entire Panhellenic system drinks, and he had a soft spot for GiGi. A little name dropping and he'd be broker than penny rollers, and he'd been there before, rolling pennies with his mom. It was the main reason he'd joined the Corps.

"Stede is going to work in security one day and wants to protect the family." GiGi recovered nicely, but revealed more than he would have.

Embry smiled and it lit up their little corner of the restaurant. "Your secret's safe with me. Now about those drinks?"

After writing down the order, she walked away, and Stede forced himself to quit staring after her. She was a sorority girl, and they were off limits. Not only had he agreed to GiGi's request to stay clear, but in his experience, they were spoiled rich girls who wanted one thing—a fraternity boy.

Now that he was out of the service, he had a new mission. Serious relationships could wait until he had his degree. Then he might be ready to find a woman and settle down. When he got married, he was gonna give it his all. It was supposed to be a lifetime commitment.

Embry came and went a few times, and he daydreamed about working with her. Since he bartended at this particular bar, chances were they'd have the same shifts during the school term. She eventually placed a burger and fries in front of him.

He cut his eyes up at her. "That's a big burger."

"It's really good." She smiled.

"I don't believe you could fit this in your mouth."

"Don't dare me because I haven't eaten today."

He leaned back in his seat and pushed the plate toward her. "I dare you."

She shook her head. "Can I get you anything else? GiGi?"

"No, I'm fine, honey," she said.

"Just one bite." He raised an eyebrow and nodded at the plate.

She huffed before she put the top bun on, squished it down, picked it up and took a huge bite.

"Miss Harris." The dining manager, a short, balding man named Bill, stood behind her.

Embry sucked in a sharp breath, and then nothing. Stede could see her throat working, trying to get air to force a cough. She put her hand on her chest and stuck her neck out like a chicken. There was no sound, but her eyes grew bigger as panic set in.

Stede stood and moved behind her, placing his hands first on her hips and encircling her with his arms as he positioned his hands for the Heimlich maneuver. He thrust in and up, picking her up off the ground and into his body.

Once was all it took. She coughed and spit food out of her mouth. He lowered her to her knees and she wretched. Bill and several other members of the wait staff moved into action. Two people carted Embry off toward the bathroom. Someone bent to clean everything up, and Bill shook his head, saying their food was on the house.

GiGi tried to cover for Embry, but Stede could see Embry's fate in the tight lines around the manager's mouth. Although he would use whatever influence he had with the boss to prevent it, the bad news was Embry might get fired and it was Stede's fault. The good news was her parents were probably rich, so she wouldn't miss the money too much.

It didn't make him feel any less guilty.

Chapter Two

As Embry dragged her heels up the front walk to the sorority house, all she could think about was getting to her room, crawling in bed, and crying herself to sleep, but one of the drawbacks of her college experience was having to share a room with someone. When you wanted privacy, like when you'd been fired from a job you didn't want to begin with, you didn't get it. On the other hand, when you wanted someone to talk to, no one was around.

Most of the girls had moved in over the weekend since rush was about to start, and the house was a beehive of activity. She had to remind herself they were trying to switch to the more formal term—recruitment.

Embry took a deep breath and pasted a smile on before she walked through the front door.

"Hey, Embry, how'd it go?" Brielle, her friend and the sorority president, asked.

"I got fired."

Several girls heard the news and after a collective gasp, they gathered around to console her and commiserate.

"You'll find something even better." Brielle hugged her. "Hey, you wanna go get a drink later? My treat."

"Sure. I'm going up to change; text me when you're ready." Embry's legs were heavy as she trod up the stairs.

She closed herself in her room and let out a sigh of relief because her roommate was out. She and her roommate had always been friends and gotten along well, but things had become tense the spring before when Chanel started dating Chase. Embry assured Chanel she didn't need to feel like her loyalties were divided since Chase had a good reason to be mad at Embry.

Shoot, she was angry with herself, too.

It seemed easier for Chanel if Embry kept her distance. Things wouldn't have been so bad if Chase hadn't wanted to share his venom with everyone he met.

As Embry changed clothes, she thought about GiGi's grandson and wondered if it was wrong to want to slap someone who'd saved your life. After all, if he hadn't dared her to eat the burger, she wouldn't have choked.

He was gorgeous, and he knew it. He'd aimed that arrogant, challenging smirk at her, and she just had to prove herself. Prove how stupid she was.

She slammed her lip gloss on the dressing table.

In some ways, she was growing up, but when she saw herself act and react like a child, she was ashamed of herself. She hadn't even said thanks. She'd have to ask GiGi how to get in touch with him and find a way to repay his kindness.

The door opened and Chanel rushed in. "Oh, my God, are you okay? Chase texted me a video of you choking at the restaurant."

"Great." Embry should've known her biggest non-fan would be quick to share her demise with the world.

"Who's the stud in the video? You can't see his face, but he has a tattoo on his very muscular arm. I can't tell what it is."

"Just a customer." Embry pulled on a denim skirt.

"What are you gonna do about a job?" Chanel sat on the edge of her bed.

"I'm not sure yet. Look around, I guess."

"It sucks that you have to work. I'd kill my parents if they limited my funds."

Embry hadn't wanted to tell the whole story about why she was working for the first time in her life, so she'd said her parents had put her on a fixed stipend to force her to be more responsible. It was actually true about the fixed sum, thus the need to supplement.

Embry buckled her sandal. "I thought about murdering them in their sleep, but I kinda like them."

There was a knock at the door, and Chanel opened it to GiGi.

"Oh, Embry." The sweet, little, old lady

opened her arms, and Embry walked into them.

Pressure was building behind her eyes, so she took a few deep breaths to try to stave the tear flow. "It's okay, GiGi."

"I'll be downstairs." Chanel closed the door on her way out.

Embry cleared her throat. "I didn't get a chance to thank your…Stede."

"He felt terrible. Told me to text him later to let him know you're okay."

Embry smiled at the memory of when she and a couple other sisters taught GiGi how to text and use the other features of her cell phone. Also, she was glad to know he was concerned since he'd nearly gotten her killed.

Okay, so maybe she hadn't accepted her part in the fiasco.

"I shouldn't have let him goad me into eating his burger."

"He was especially sorry for antagonizing you. He cuts up a lot and never meant for you to get hurt."

"It was good he knew how to save me then."

"He's a hero, my Stede." GiGi put her fingers on her lips. "I've got to stop saying things like that. I'm just so proud of him. He's going to the technical college to get his degree, and then he's gonna do some fancy government job because of his military background."

Embry patted her arm. "You have every right to be proud. You tell him, not only that I said thanks for saving me, but thanks for his service. My dad was a Marine. Served in Vietnam. So I know what it's like to be proud of someone like that."

"You're a good girl. He's going to try to help with your job situation. He knows the boss."

Embry shrugged and smiled. "That's okay. I kinda stunk at the job. He might not want to go out on a limb for me."

GiGi squeezed her hand. "That's what he does, goes out on limbs for people. Plus, he works there too."

Embry's jaw came unhinged for a second. "What the what?"

* * *

Stede stood behind the bar and watched the baseball game on ESPN. He'd offered to bartend since Embry had been let go, and they needed another waitress on the floor. When he heard a gaggle of women come in the door, he knew without looking they were sorority girls. A quick glance over his shoulder confirmed his suspicion, but a second look was warranted because Embry was among them. Next to her, the other girls were trolls. He should look away and was about to when she caught him staring. She smiled, and when her friends turned his way, she directed them to a table.

Pete moved to stand closer to Stede, while he dried a glass. "I need to get her alone, so I can talk to her."

"What do you want me to do about it?" Stede asked.

"Motion her over here, if you can get her attention." Pete slung the towel over his shoulder.

Since her back was to the bar, Stede didn't think she wanted to see him, much less come over for a chat. He was surprised she was there at all.

"You be careful of those pretty girls." Pete nodded toward the group.

"You don't have to worry about me." Stede had already resisted advances from a few of the waitresses, including Michelle who doubled as a bartender at times. His mom had told him not to fish off both sides of the company pier.

"Some of these girls nowadays—they get prettier and their morals get looser." Pete ran a hand through his salt and pepper hair.

"That's a good thing for the guys around here, I guess." Stede dusted the bottles on display.

"Yeah, but have you considered one of those girls might be your future wife? How's it make you feel knowing she's been had by every fraternity boy who bought her a drink?"

"Not good, but chances are none of those girls will ever look twice at me, and I sure as hell can't afford to maintain them in the lifestyle to which they've become accustomed. That knocks me out of the running for husband of the year."

The door opened and a crew of fraternity boys came in. They moved tables to combine with the girls, and Stede purposely made himself watch the baseball game.

"Hey, barkeep," one of the guys approached the bar, wallet in hand, "let me get a couple of pitchers of beer and some cups." He dropped a twenty on the counter.

While Pete pulled two pitchers, the frat boy eyed Stede. "Hey, guy, don't I know you?"

Stede glanced the guy's way after he placed the

cups on the bar. "Don't think so."

"Do you go to school with us?"

"No."

"You look so familiar. I'm Chase Clayborne." He held his hand out.

"Stede Bennett."

"No freaking way. Like the pirate?"

Stede gritted his teeth and tried not to show his irritation. He loved his mom, but why she'd named him after the gentleman pirate, he'd never understand. "That's Stede Bonnet."

"Sure, it is. Dude, I'm from Charleston. I think I know my hometown pirate's name. Bonnet, yeah right. I swear I know you from somewhere though. I'll think of it." He pulled out his phone. "Hey, have y'all seen this?"

Stede already thought Chase was an idiot, but he'd just proven it. Not only was the last name Bonnet, the man was from Barbados; although, he did die in Charleston. He'd hung for piracy and related crimes.

Chase shoved the phone toward Stede. Pete had two full pitchers of beer ready to go, but he leaned over to also look at the screen. It was a video of Stede and Embry, during and after the incident that could have killed her. Guilt punched him in the gut.

Pete pointed. "Isn't that?"

Stede caught his eye and shook his head.

"Yeah, she's the biggest tease on campus. Serves the bitch right."

"What did she ever do to you?" Pete asked.

"It's what she didn't do, if you know what I mean." Chase pushed the twenty toward Pete and picked up the beer. "Keep the change."

"Much obliged." Pete took the money to the register.

Stede had a moment to think about what Chase had said. He couldn't imagine anyone deserving to choke to death for being a tease. Embry must have embarrassed the frat boy in a major way for him to say something so harsh. Then again, he might just be a dirtbag.

As if he'd said it out loud, Pete approached. "Don't listen to that guy. I shouldn't say this because he tips so well, but he's a creep."

"I kinda figured." Stede replaced several fifths of liquor on the wall.

"When you talked me into re-hiring that little girl, you didn't tell me the whole story." Pete gave Stede a knowing look before he pulled another beer.

"Now that you know, you changing your mind?"

"Nah, she's a nice girl. I'll give her another chance." Pete wiped down the bar.

While Stede mixed drinks and pulled beers, he thought about that little girl. She'd felt more like a woman when he'd had his hands on her, but he hadn't gotten to enjoy that part of the process. A do-over situation without the near death and vomit might be nice.

The sound of cheering drew his attention. The fraternity boys were having a chugging contest. When it was over, Chase and another guy chest bumped. Everyone at the table stood and Chase put his arm around a blonde while the crew made their way to the door. Stede turned back to the television, so he wouldn't have to see Embry walk out with some guy drooling all over her. The bar got quiet when the door closed behind them.

"Hey, can I get a drink?"

He glanced over his shoulder to see Embry and immediately returned his attention to the game. "You twenty-one?"

"Of course. You owe me one."

He turned and propped his elbows on the bar. "How do you figure? The way I see it, you should be buying me a drink."

"Why?" She tried not to smile. "To thank you for getting me fired?"

He raised an eyebrow. "Fired is better than dead."

"I can't argue with that." Embry reached into the back pocket of her mini skirt and fanned three ones on the bar. "I'll have to get you the two dollar draft."

Stede almost felt a little sorry for her since she'd run out of allowance so early in the semester. Finance probably wasn't her major and money management wasn't a high priority for sorority girls, as far as he knew.

According to his friends, he was a tightwad. While he was getting his regular military and hazard pay for his deployments, he'd saved everything he could after sending money home to his mom and GiGi. With his Post 911 G.I. Bill benefits, he figured he'd have enough to live on while working a part-time job for the four years it took him to get his degree. Another look at Embry and he thought about giving her private lessons on how to live within her means.

He grinned. "I don't drink on the job."

Pete walked up beside him. "And I think Embry's learned her lesson about eating on the job. You okay, kid?"

Her cheeks turned pink, and she dipped her head down. "Yes, sir."

"I think Bill might have overreacted earlier. I'd like you to come in to work tomorrow."

Her eyes grew wide. "Really?"

Pete pointed at her and tilted his head. "No more eating customer's food."

"Deal…but technically, he's not a customer. He's a plant you put there to spy on me."

Pete put his hands up in surrender. "Just doing his old boss a favor."

"Way to throw me under the bus, boss man." Stede patted Pete's back.

"It's almost closing time, kids. Can I put in a food order for you? Employees eat free."

Stede happened to be looking at Embry when she sucked in a deep breath. "I was afraid to eat after my near death experience. By the way, I'm sorry if I threw up on you."

He wasn't planning to bring it up. "Don't worry about it."

"You need to eat. What'll you have?" Pete asked.

"Anything but the burger." She gave Stede a pointed look.

Stede crossed his arms over his chest. "I'll take the burger since I didn't get to enjoy mine."

When Pete had gone, she sat on a barstool. "I

know I can't fully repay you, unless I jump on a grenade or something to save you, but I could buy you a beer to go with your burger. Do you want it?"

"No, keep your money. I'm driving."

"GiGi said you were smart." She smiled and his heart might have skipped a beat. "Hey, did Chase tip you guys?"

"Yeah, he took care of Pete." He grabbed a cup. "What are you drinking?"

"Coke. No, make that Diet Coke."

"Why?"

"I have my reasons."

"They're not because you need to lose weight."

"Just being proactive."

Pete returned. "Food will be ready soon."

Embry took a sip of her diet drink and shuddered.

"Do we need to add syrup?" Pete asked.

Embry shook her head. "It's diet."

"Didn't you tell me you dieted most of the summer to get ready for your sister's wedding?" Pete took her cup and gave her another. "Give yourself a break. Drink the real thing. A little meat on your bones won't kill you. Tell her, Stede."

"Man's got a point." Stede did not want to get dragged into this discussion.

Embry said, "The guys at school think thinner is better."

"Those guys are morons." Stede spoke before he could stop himself.

"Well, don't you go hurrying to get married. You got a lot of living to do," Pete said. "That's both your sisters married now, isn't it?"

"Yes, sir. I'm not in a hurry. I'm thinking of freaking my parents out and shacking up with someone for a while."

Pete laughed and waved his bar towel at her. "Girl, you ain't right."

"That's what they keep telling me." She grinned.

"Listen," Pete leaned on the counter, "in case you didn't know, there's a video of—"

She put her hand up. "I know. I honestly don't remember a time when I didn't have a cell phone, but about now I wish I lived in the eighties."

Pete nodded and moved away to close out a tab.

"That why you're trying to bring back the denim mini skirt?" Stede asked.

"You." She swatted at him. "I've decided I'm not letting you push my buttons. It almost got me killed already."

Stede wanted to push a lot more than her buttons. "Yeah, I'm sorry about that."

She waved her hand. "My fault." She rubbed her forehead. "I didn't tell anyone it was you. They noticed your tattoo, but I don't think they can tell what it is."

The sleeve of his work T-shirt covered the skull and cross-daggers tattoo on his upper arm, but it showed a little in his own shirts. He rubbed the area as he went to lock the front door and turn off some of the lights. When he got back to the bar, Pete had set his plate next to Embry's.

She had a mouthful of food when she spoke. "Don't let me eat all this or I won't be able to walk."

He slid onto the stool next to her. "Where you walking to?"

"Back to the house."

"Why didn't you ride with your friends?"

"They were going to Chase's house, and I'm not exactly welcome."

"You must've left him brokenhearted?"

She shrugged. "If he had a heart, I might agree with you. Insulted his pride, more like."

He turned on his seat to face her. "Oh? Do tell."

"Not on your life."

Embry was a vault. He wondered how hard she'd be to crack.

Chapter Three

Embry dipped her chicken fingers and french fries in ranch dressing, enjoying every delicious high-calorie bite. So much for not gaining weight. She'd do better tomorrow. She had her job back, and that was a relief, as well as a source of stress.

She glanced at her dining companion and smiled to herself. They weren't exactly alone. Several other staff members were seated down the bar for what they called midnight breakfast. It wasn't breakfast food, and it was way past midnight, but who was she to point out the obvious?

She thought she was getting a vibe from Stede, but it'd been a long time since she'd gotten male attention. She might be misreading the situation. He was the best looking guy she'd ever seen not on the cover of a magazine, so she was more than a little tempted. Especially since she'd been at the health clinic that morning and gotten her first quarterly birth control shot. But, she wasn't ready to test it out yet. As staunch Catholics, her parents would kill her if they knew. That's why they never would.

If she could do one thing to end her college experience on a positive note, it would be to get a boyfriend and have a lot of sex. Preferably with a fraternity boy who adored her, which the guy beside her wasn't. Everyone would know because there were no secrets in the Greek Village. Her reputation as a tease would be refuted, once and for all.

Her phone buzzed and she nearly cussed the thing. It was a SnapChat photo of Chanel on Chase's lap. Topless. Thankfully, the image would disappear after ten seconds. Embry thought about throwing her arm around Stede and taking her own selfie, since the girls had drooled over him when they'd seen him behind the bar earlier. But she refrained and slid her phone into her back pocket.

She sipped her Coke. One of the side effects of her birth control was weight gain, and despite what Pete and Stede said, she didn't think extra pounds would help her attract a boyfriend. Hence, the main reason she hadn't eaten all day.

She wiped her mouth and placed her napkin on her plate. "Thanks, Pete."

"I'll take that." Pete reached across the bar and took the plate from her.

"I'll see you guys tomorrow."

"Wait a second." Stede caught her arm. "I can't let you walk home by yourself at this hour."

"I walk all over the place by myself."

"If you get raped and killed, I'll never forgive myself."

"Okay, now I'm scared. Thanks for that. Do

you have a savior complex?"

"Only around you."

He was good. Too damn good. Nobody, no guy, said stuff like that and meant it. "Are you the type of savior who rescues the damsel from the trouble you create?"

His grin sent a jolt of excitement through her.

"I can see why you might think that, but no, I'm a responsible adult." He stood. "Now, how 'bout I give you a ride?"

"How adult are you?"

He tilted his head to the side and raised his eyebrows. "You're a flirty little thing."

"I was asking your age, not how X-rated you can get. You're a guy. I already know the answer to that one."

"Nice recovery, sorority girl. I'm twenty-two, and you might not want to lump all guys in one general category. While it's true we think with our little heads much of the time, some of us are capable of being nice about it."

All the right words. His smooth talking probably worked on every woman he met. Combined with his pale blue eyes and chiseled features, it was a deadly combo. The truth was, he made her nervous, not because she was afraid he would hurt her, but because there was an attraction she hadn't let herself feel in a long time.

"You coming or not?" He walked toward the door.

She looked up at him, pulled from her thoughts. "I guess."

He held the door open for her. A lot of boys in

the south did that, but Embry didn't see it as much as she used to.

She needed Stede to *not* hit on her and his name gave her an idea. "I hate to ask this, but your last name's not Bonnet, is it?"

He smiled and she wished he'd stop it. There was a lot of wattage behind that smile, and his mouth was sexy.

"It's Bennett. My mom played a cruel joke when she named me." He ran his hand through his hair. "At least, she tried to raise me to be a gentleman."

"Yeah, but he kinda sucked at being a pirate. He turned his ships over to Blackbeard because he couldn't command his men."

"Mom didn't care about that stuff. When I was old enough to learn all about him, I wondered if she picked the name because my dad decided he didn't love her anymore and left us. Bonnet took up pirating to get away from a bad marriage."

"I can't imagine a mother would do that. Plus, most people don't know the details. It just sounds cool to say you were named after the *Gentleman Pirate*."

"You remind me of an island girl."

She scrunched her nose. "Thanks, I think. I guess pirates are known for hanging around islands."

He grinned. "And stealing the girls."

"I'll keep that in mind." Her skin tingled. "My mom is of Spanish descent. That's where we get the dark hair and skin. My mom and sisters are gorgeous."

"Who told you that you weren't?"

She shrugged and rolled her shoulders inward. "No one had to."

He stopped walking and turned her to face him. Placing a finger under her chin, he opened his mouth to speak. He closed it and waited a beat before he asked, "Are you fishing for compliments?"

"Uh, no. Do you think you're handsome?"

"I don't think I'm ugly. What do you think?"

"You know you're smokin' and I don't think I'm ugly either. I'm just not as pretty as the other women in my family."

"Since I've never met the other women in your family, I can't agree or disagree with you, but I can tell you you're the best looking woman I've seen since moving home."

Her cheeks got warm and she tried to look down, but his finger was still under her chin, holding her head in place. "Thanks. You too." It sounded dumb to her own ears, like when someone working at a hotel says enjoy your stay and you say, "You too." *Ridiculous.*

He turned and walked a few steps before he swung his leg over a motorcycle. "Here we are."

"Um, this is how you're planning to take me home?"

"It's the only ride I've got."

When she'd nearly died earlier, she'd only eaten a bite of a burger. It wasn't like she was flirting with disaster, but a motorcycle was like inviting death.

She took a step back. "I'm sorry, but I can't

ride with you."

"Why not? Chicken?"

She hated being called a chicken, but she'd learned something about herself earlier and she was going with the adult reaction of caution. "For starters, my parents would kill me."

"Do you tell your parents everything you do?"

"No." She put her hands on her hips. "But getting on that bike with you, considering I almost bit the big one earlier, might not be in my best interest."

"Do you think I'd save your life just to put you in danger? I'm a safe driver, and I'm a little insulted you'd think I'm not."

"Liar. You're not insulted. I can tell by your smirk you're messing with me." She motioned her arm to her outfit. "I'm wearing a skirt."

His gaze moved from her eyes down to her toes and back up again. "I don't see the problem."

The heat in his look made her sweat. Or, it might have been the warm August night. She put her hands on her hips. "What about helmets?"

"Don't need one if you're twenty-one. It's not far and I'll go slow. Cross my heart." He made the gesture.

She sucked in her cheek and chewed on it while she thought. She'd never been on a motorcycle. He started the engine and her body vibrated from the proximity to the rumbling motor. It was an exciting feeling, and she wanted to be on the bike, closer to the source of the sound.

After using the hair band on her wrist to tie her hair back, she rested one hand on his arm while she pulled up the side of her skirt and lifted her leg over the bike. She found the foot rests and squirmed to settle onto the padded leather seat.

He put on a pair of yellow tinted glasses and spoke over his shoulder. "Hold on to me with your hands and knees."

He placed one of his hands on her knee where it rested against his hip and the other on her hand, which rested on his abdomen. The combination of his touch, his big warm body, and the rumble under her butt sent a rush of blood and lust through her veins. She flattened her palms against his torso and felt the hard lines and ridges beneath his thin T-shirt. She made herself stop feeling him up and locked her arms together.

He looked down before he twisted slightly to see her. He wore a wicked grin. "Don't smile or you might get bugs in your teeth."

She laughed and leaned her cheek against his back. When they began to move, the rush of wind in her ears drowned out every thought and every fear. She closed her eyes and let her head fall back, keeping her arms tight around his body.

Embry had never experienced that kind of rush, where she let herself be in the moment. Her heart was light, and she slowly pressed her knees tighter against him and let one arm fall out by her side, then the other.

They came to an intersection where he was about to turn toward campus.

"Do we have to go straight back?" She bit her lip.

He looked over his shoulder. "Do I have a

natural born rider on my bike?"

She answered by squeezing his shoulders, and he turned the other way. They rode for a while, crisscrossing the river. The streets were quiet in the wee hours of the night. She'd never felt freer, so she opened her arms wide and reveled in the sensation of flight.

They stopped at the park by the river. He cut the engine, put down the bike stand, and removed his glasses. "Well, what do you think?"

Her heart was still racing, and she slid back a little on the seat to give him some space. "You're a good driver."

"I mean about the ride."

"I've never felt anything like it."

He got off the bike and offered her his hand. "Clears your head, doesn't it?"

She smiled because he understood. She didn't think she could explain it, but she didn't need to, not to him.

He walked down to the water, and she followed before she realized she was acting like a puppy running after someone who might give her attention. She stopped and hung back.

He turned. "What's wrong? You're not afraid of me, are you?"

She hadn't thought she should be afraid until he asked. She gave herself a mental kick for letting herself go off in the dark with a guy she barely knew. She looked at him again and let herself off the hook. Her gut told her he was good. And so did Gigi.

He moved toward her, but not in a threatening

way. "You're smart to be cautious, Embry. Not because I'm dangerous, but because not all men can be trusted."

He was within arm's reach, and she held his gaze. "I know, but *you* can be."

"So, do you want to go for a ride with me this weekend? I'll bring helmets."

"Can't. It's rush, I mean, recruitment, so when I'm not working, I'll be knee deep in sorority sisters and recruits."

"Sounds like a bad place to be. Like a herd of heifers."

She laughed and inched closer. "You better not let them hear you say that."

"Notwithstanding my mode of transportation, I don't have a death wish." He grinned. "Besides, you're one of them."

She looked down at her feet. She'd been on the outside for too long, fighting to hang on to a little acceptance. Despite paying her dues and showing up, she hadn't considered herself one of them in quite a while. She was still friends with a lot of the girls, but there was a chasm between her and the rest of the world.

He put a finger under her chin and lifted her head. "When you look sad like that, it makes me want to kiss you."

Chapter Four

Stede didn't know what alien had taken over his brain and forced him to speak without thinking. He'd been imagining kissing her since she'd decided to get on his bike. He'd watched with an eagerness that was foreign to him as she'd hiked her skirt up and settled in behind him. Between her breasts on his back, her hands on his stomach, and her knees on his hips, he was thoroughly turned on. Being the good guy was really difficult at times.

"Stede, I, um, I feel it too, but I don't think we should. I hope you don't think I've been leading you on."

He was the idiot who'd made the first move, and he couldn't let her berate herself. He lightly gripped her upper arms. "I hit on you, not the other way around. I shouldn't have. You're off limits."

"Off limits like how?"

He let go of her arms and ran a hand through his hair. "A hundred ways."

"Can't we be friends?

"We'll be working together. Friendly, but not friends."

She raised her eyebrows and tilted her head. "Secret friends? At least an occasional ride on your fat boy? Wait." She held up a hand. "That came out wrong. I didn't mean…you know?"

He laughed and dropped his head forward. He definitely wanted to give her a ride on his *fat boy*, but he'd have to pass.

He checked his watch. "I've got to get you back. The sun will be coming up soon, and I have class in a few hours."

"I'm sorry. You should've said something earlier. Let's go." She walked back to the bike and hesitated. "I guess you have to get on first."

Damn, she was gorgeous. He made himself get on the bike, instead of pulling her in for a kiss. Once he got her back to the sorority house, that would be the end of their alone time. Sure, he'd have to interact with her at work, but she'd do her Greek thing and forget all about him. It was for the best because she tempted him beyond his good sense.

He took the shortest route back to campus and tried to memorize her body as she held onto him.

He pulled off to the side of the street before they got to the Greek Village and turned to speak to her. "I'm not lingering once we get there. Get off and get inside. If anyone sees us, don't tell them anything about me."

"That won't be hard. I don't know anything about you, besides where you work, you were named for a pirate, and you think I'm an island girl." She smiled. "Oh, you're also good to have around if I choke." She kissed his cheek. "Thank you for that and thank you for the ride. It's such a rush."

Her lips sent a rush straight to his groin, enough so that he had to shift on the seat. He drove on and dropped her in front of the massive Greek revival style house. When she dismounted, he drove away slowly and watched in his mirror until she disappeared inside.

Unbeknownst to her, Embry didn't let him get any sleep.

He'd have to take measures to get her out of his head. It was a mistake to lay it on the line with her. He never thought he'd be thankful for Fall Rush, but he was.

* * *

The next day, Embry went in for the lunch shift and was disappointed to discover Stede wasn't supposed to be in until later. She couldn't stop thinking about him and kicking herself for not letting him kiss her. His lips were perfectly full, and she bet he knew how to use them.

The day was going well, despite her mind being only partially engaged in work. Where she wanted to be was on the back of a motorcycle with her arms around Stede.

"What can I get you fellas to drink?" She poised her pen over the ticket book.

"Hey, Embry." Mark Peterson was one of the few Tappa Kegs who was nice to her, as long as Chase wasn't around.

"Hey, you ready for rush?" she asked.

"Yeah. This is my cousin, Griffin. I'm courting him because he's a Tri Mu legacy."

"Tough choice, but good luck figuring it out. What are you drinking?"

They ordered and when she walked away, she smiled at Griffin's parting comment. "You were right about the pretty girls, cuz."

When she delivered their drinks and took their food order, Griffin asked, "Are you going to the First Night party?"

"I plan to, if I don't have to work."

"Maybe I'll see you there."

She started to tell him there'd be so many people it was unlikely, but she smiled and nodded instead. After they'd paid their bill and were about to leave, Griffin found Embry at the drink station.

"You wanna go out with me sometime?" He stood sideways to her and tucked his thumbs in his front pockets.

Clearly, he hadn't heard about her yet, or he wouldn't be asking. It had been so long since someone had asked her out she was tempted to say yes just so she could say she had a date, but he was a freshman. No post-graduation potential there.

She'd never dated a younger guy, but it might be time to start. "I'll have to check my schedule, but yeah, that'd be nice."

He exhaled and let out a nervous laugh. "Thank goodness. I thought you were about to turn me down." He kicked his shoe against the floor. "Can I get your number?"

She told him the number as he entered it in his

phone.

"Looks like the little princess has a date." Michelle nudged her with her elbow. She was one of the long-time waitresses who'd trained Embry.

"That's okay, right? I won't get in trouble for giving him my number, will I?"

"Girl, I've been working here for ten years and wished a young lady-killer would ask for my number." She filled a cup with ice. "Been trying to slip my number to Stede the Stud, but he doesn't date co-workers."

Embry's smile faded.

"I know, right?" Michelle pressed the cup against the lever of the Coke dispenser. "You're a double negative because he also doesn't date sorority girls."

Embry had assumed the reason she was off-limits was because GiGi was her house mother, but it looked like Stede had a whole list of reasons after all. She didn't understand why the news disappointed her so much. He fit none of the criteria on the list for potential mate material she'd established, apart from being male and easy on the eyes.

"Sounds like you've got the low down." Embry forced the corners of her mouth up.

"You need the 411, you come see me."

Embry laughed and shook her head.

"What? Are we not saying that anymore?"

"Not in many years." Embry took a pitcher of sweet tea to go check her tables for refills.

While she worked, her mind kept revisiting the previous night. Stede had kind of asked her out. He must have temporarily forgotten his rules. She smiled and wondered if she could get him to forget again. She'd never been the type of person who enjoyed a challenge, but there was some appeal to this one. The bartender had his own plans and so did she.

Chapter Five

Stede looked for Embry when he got to work, but Michelle told him she had a sorority thing. Michelle liked to catch him up on the staff gossip, so he listened patiently while he worked. He learned Embry's nickname was *Princess* and someone had asked her out and she hadn't said no. The news made his chest tighten, but he got over it when he decided he'd go to a bar near the Army base and get a date of his own on his next night off.

He motioned for Pete to cover for him while he took a bathroom break. Both urinals were occupied, so he pushed open one of the stall doors with his foot and walked in, letting it slam behind him. The noise from the bar invaded the space each time the door opened and closed. He was about to flush when he heard a female voice in the next stall.

"What do you want, Chase?"

Stede's ears perked up. He didn't recognize the girl's voice, but the guy's belonged to the Chase he'd met the day before.

"I need a favor. The bartender. All the girls say he's hot. Do you agree?"

"Oh, hell yeah."

"Good. Then you won't have a problem getting to know him better."

"It'd be my pleasure." She giggled. "What's this about?"

"I'm thinking about recruiting him."

Stede quietly worked his zipper up and buttoned his jeans.

"You mean to join your fraternity?"

"No, Carol Anne, he doesn't even go to our school. I need help with a project."

"So, what do you want me to find out from him?"

Stede shifted his feet.

"Is he straight? Does he need a friend like me? Can he be trusted?"

"No problem."

"That's a good girl." Sloppy kissing noises filled the air. "Now, while I've got you here, why don't you do me another favor?" The distinct sound of a zipper going down came from the next stall.

"What about Chanel?"

"I won't tell if you won't."

When the outer door opened, Stede made his escape. He went straight back to the bar and washed his hands there, trying to make sense of what he'd overheard. He had to be the guy they were talking about, and Chase wanted to recruit him for a project. Stede's first instinct was Chase might be looking for a scapegoat.

He had two choices. He could shoot the girl down and send her packing, or he could see how things played out. The latter was tempting because he wanted to know what Chase was up to.

Sooner than he thought possible, based on seeing knees on the bathroom floor under the stall door, a bosomy brunette slinked up to the bar.

He propped his hands on the bar and leaned forward. "What can I get you?"

She twirled her hair. "You buying?"

"No."

"In that case, maybe I can interest you in something?" She ran a finger down the center of her chest.

"I don't date sorority girls."

She smacked her gum. "Who said anything about dating?" Her eyes drifted down his body.

"Why don't you tell me what it is that you want?" He shifted to give her a better view and flexed with intent.

Her eyes fixed on his chest before she extended her hand. "I'm Carol Anne."

He was pretty sure he knew where her hand had recently been, so he crossed his arms over his chest. "And?"

"Are you gay?"

He grinned. "No."

"You wanna take me back to your place?"

"Can't," he hesitated until she pouted, "tonight."

She smiled and dropped her hand from her hair, letting it graze her chest on the way down. "So, would you like a new friend?"

"I could always use a *friend*."

"Can I trust you to keep it a secret?"

"Why?"

"Because the fraternity brothers don't like it when we date outside the Greek Village." She twirled her hair.

"Protective, huh? I could use friends like that. And, baby, I can definitely keep a secret." He flashed her his best sexy look.

If he were the bragging type, he'd tell everyone how she swooned and giggled like a schoolgirl.

"You should go back to your friends before they see you talking to me and get suspicious."

"Oh, good idea. See you around."

It didn't escape his notice that she'd asked him to take her home, but she hadn't asked his name. It was about a half hour until last call and most of the college crowd filtered out of the bar. Carol Anne blew him a kiss as she left.

Before they were all gone, Chase came to the bar. "Pirate guy. What's up?"

"Not much, Greek guy. Y'all having a good time?" Stede kept his eyes on the bar as he wiped it down.

"Always, man. Listen, I have a little wager for you. Want to make a hundred bucks?"

Stede thought it was typical for a guy like Chase to think Stede could be bought because he didn't come from money. "What did you have in mind?"

"See, there's this girl. She's locked up tighter than Fort Knox."

"Who? Carol Anne?"

"No, no, not her. Another girl."

"How do you know she's locked up, as you say?" Stede raised an eyebrow.

"Man, she got me completely naked and left me there, high and dry. Total cock tease."

Stede suspected he knew who Chase meant. "Did she take your clothes and leave you to get home naked?"

"No, she just changed her mind. She was naked too."

"Maybe the size of your junk scared her." Stede tried not to laugh.

Chase paused and looked off into the distance for a moment. "If I were the only guy she did it to, I might agree with you."

Stede wondered how many more there were.

"So, what is it you need from me?" Stede asked.

"I'll give you a hundred bucks if you can get into her pants."

"Why me?"

"She doesn't trust me or my brothers."

"What makes you think she'll trust me?"

"You're an outsider, but you still have access to her. She works here."

Stede narrowed his eyes.

"The girls find you attractive. Embry might too."

"What kind of name is that?" Stede relaxed his hands, which had fisted at his sides.

"I'm surprised you haven't met her."

"Different shifts."

"The name is…you know, like Embry-Riddle?

The aviation school?"

"Ah." Stede nodded his head. He was fairly sure his island girl hadn't been named for that. "If I agree to this, what proof do you need? So, I can get my hundred bucks."

"Video."

"So, you expect me to get a girl, whom you refer to as Fort Knox, to have sex with me and let me video it?"

"She doesn't have to know you're videoing it."

"Isn't that illegal?"

"No one will know but you and me."

Sure, I believe that.

Chase extended his hand. "Do we have a deal?"

Stede looked at his offered hand for a long moment. If Chase thought he'd do it, maybe it would keep him from recruiting someone else for the job. "Deal."

Chase turned to go, but stopped and looked back. "And, in case you thought it would be easy, I have a few other guys on the job. A little competition might speed things along."

Stede wanted nothing more than to rip Chase's head from his shoulders, but he stood calmly and watched him walk away. When he was gone, Stede searched the bar for Embry. Earlier, Michelle had told him she'd come in with a group of girls, but he'd shown disinterest at the time.

He found her in a corner with a guy. His arm was on the back of her chair, and he was pulling out all the stops, leaning in, touching her hair, making eye contact. Embry was engaged in conversation with him, so Stede kept an eye on the corner while he worked to clean behind the bar.

When she got up, she swayed on her feet, and the guy steadied her. She made her way through the tables by holding onto chairs and went down the hall to the bathroom. She was drunk. The guy stayed at the table, so Stede went to the hall to wait. When Embry came out, she ran into him.

He put his arms around her. "Having a nice night, Princess?"

She looked up at him and smiled before she rested her head on his chest. "I feel funny."

Chapter Six

Embry stretched and rolled onto her back before she opened her eyes. Within seconds, her heartbeat thundered in her ears and her stomach roiled as panic set in. She wasn't in her bed.

She clutched the covers to her chest and sat up, despite the pounding in her head. The full size bed was pushed into a corner of the small room. Near the foot of the bed sat a desk and chair. To the right was a small kitchen. There was no dining table, just a short bar with two stools. On the wall opposite the bed was a couch made of brown plaid circa 1970. On the couch was a guy, asleep with his back to her. He was fully clothed.

She let out a long slow breath. She lowered the covers to find she was still dressed, except for her bra. She leaned a little to peer at the floor beside the bed. Sure enough, her bra lay there next to her shoes. It was the place she always deposited those items if she went to sleep tired or drunk. She leaned over to retrieve the heavily padded lace and spandex booby trap before the sleeping man discovered she was a boob fraud. It was a tricky proposition to make As look like large Bs, but thanks to Victoria and her secrets, it was doable. She should be more concerned about waking up in a strange place with no memory of how she got there than boobage, but the fact that the guy wasn't naked in bed with her calmed her thundering heart.

The bed creaked and moaned when she moved and the guy on the couch shifted. She grabbed the bra and returned to her seated position, groping for the covers to pull up over her chest again.

"Mornin', Princess." Stede yawned as he sat up and scratched his stubble before he ran a hand through his unruly hair.

Her shoulders fell away from her ears, and she took a deep breath. Damn, he looked sexy when he woke up, but Embry was still confused about where she was and how she'd gotten there.

"Good morning." She bit her lip, wondering how to phrase her question. "How did I…? Why am I…? Where…?"

She covered her face with her hand and felt pressure behind her eyes. Thinking back to the previous night, a bunch of them had gone out for a drink after orientation. There was a new guy who showed a lot of interest and promise, not the freshman, but a transfer student from a rival school.

His name was Trent and the guys gave him hell about doing his first three years with the enemy, but he was a brother, so he was welcomed at the same time.

Embry remembered thinking it was a good day because two new guys flirted with her. This morning, she was wary.

"How much did you drink last night?" Stede was seated on the couch, watching her.

"Like a beer and a half. At least, that's all I remember drinking."

"Who was the guy?"

She told him the basics.

"Why'd he transfer?"

She shrugged. "Change of heart? I dunno."

"Could he have slipped you something?"

"Why would he?"

He raised an eyebrow and shook his head before he stood and went to the bathroom. She knew what he was thinking, but the guy was cute and charming. He wouldn't need to drug a girl to get her into bed. In her case, he would've had to take her out a few times to make sure they connected, but she would've dated him.

She took Stede's absence as the opportunity she needed to put her bra on.

He came out just as she got the last strap in place. He grinned before he moved into the small kitchen. "You hungry?"

He turned his back to her and stuck his head in the refrigerator. She made a minor cup adjustment and got out of bed.

He held up a carton of eggs. "I make a mean egg sandwich."

Her stomach growled. She hadn't eaten since breakfast the day before; partly because of lack of time and partly because of her desire to not gain weight.

"I'd love one. I need to borrow your bathroom and then I'll help."

"Be sure to put it back."

"Put what back?"

"The bathroom." He smirked.

She laughed. "You sound like my Paw-Paw."

"My Pops used to say that too." He held up a cast iron skillet. "How do you want your egg?"

"Over easy."

He curled his lip. "Disgusting."

* * *

When Embry came out of the bathroom and joined him in the kitchen, the smell of mint filled Stede's nostrils.

He cut his eyes to her. "You didn't use my toothbrush, did ya?"

"I hope it's okay. I only dropped it in the toilet once, but I rinsed it in hot water afterward." She pressed her lips together to contain her smile.

He grabbed the pencil on the fridge and jotted on his grocery list: *toothbrush*.

Her laughter lightened his heavy heart. He didn't know how to tell her about Chase and his diabolical plan to destroy her. At least, that's how Stede viewed it. He needed Embry to tell him what had really happened and why, so he could keep her safe. She needed to know what she was up against, but Stede couldn't think of how to tell her without hurting her pride. Of course, better her pride now than her life later.

The toast popped out of the toaster, and Embry put the pieces on a plate and inserted two more.

Before she pushed the lever down, she asked, "You do want yours toasted, right?"

"Yeah. Go ahead and take the first two slices. Your egg's about ready."

She looked at the butter next to the plate. "Do you have any mayo?"

He turned his head to look at her. "Mayo on an egg sandwich? Gross." He winked. "Check the fridge."

"It's really good. You should try it."

He enjoyed the view while she bent to retrieve the mayonnaise from the door of the fridge. The fitted shirt and skinny jeans revealed more than she probably thought they did. She got her bread ready, and he slid the egg on it. She used the knife to cut the sandwich into four small squares. Egg yolk spread across the plate, and he scrunched his nose until she caught him.

"It's good. You should try it."

He shook his head. "No, thanks."

"The best part is using the edges of the bread to scoop up the yolk. Yum." She poured two cups of coffee from the tiny coffee pot and bumped into him as she turned to set them on the bar. "Sorry."

"Welcome to the world's smallest kitchen."

"In the world's smallest apartment." She grinned as she picked up her plate. "I'm so jealous. I'd give anything to have my own space."

"It's kinda nice. Especially after barracks and CHUs."

"What's a chew?" she asked before biting into a square of her sandwich.

"Containerized Housing Unit." He cracked two

eggs into the skillet and scrambled them.

When his toast popped up, Embry wiped her hands on her paper towel and put the bread slices on his plate. "Do you want me to butter these?"

"I'm tempted to try it with mayo, but just a little."

She smiled as she dressed his toast. Then she held the plate while he scraped the eggs from the pan onto the bread. "You want me to cut it for you?"

"No one has cut my sandwiches for me since grade school." At her look of disappointment, he added, "Go ahead."

She did and placed his plate next to his coffee cup while he soaked the skillet. They both moved to the stools on the other side of the bar.

"Were you scared over there?" she asked.

"Sometimes. Especially my first deployment, but once you get used to it and know what to expect, it's not so bad." He didn't want to talk about it. "Why do they call you Princess?"

"Oh, that. Well, when Pete hired me, he said he'd work around my classes and sorority stuff. Recently, he asked about rush, and I started telling him about orientation and all of the events I am supposed to attend until I noticed several of the wait staff were listening. I didn't ask for special treatment."

"You don't want to attend your sorority events?"

"No, I wanted to quit, but my parents wouldn't let me, even though it strapped them financially."

"Why quit?"

"My experience hasn't met the expectations I came to school with. Freshman year did, but things changed after that." She ran her finger around the edge of her plate.

"What happened?"

She sipped her coffee and bit her lip before she turned to look out the window of the exterior door. "I did something stupid."

He decided it was time to share what he knew about it. "Does it have anything to do with a certain asshole named Chase?"

She turned to look at him. "Yeah." She let out a long breath. "To hear him tell it, I slept with every brother freshman year and came back sophomore year to leave every one of them naked with nothing to show for it."

"What's the real story?"

She put the last bite of her sandwich in her mouth. "I dated two guys freshman year, not at the same time. It wasn't serious, but it wasn't one-night stand situations either." She pinched the bridge of her nose. "My sister, Indi, got married to her college sweetheart the summer between my freshman and sophomore years. After the wedding, they told us she was pregnant. They'd had a condom incident. The next time I found myself naked with a guy, I panicked. All I could think about was a leak and me facing a difficult choice. Indi and Cobie were in a committed relationship, and I wasn't, so the whole single mother path stretched out in my mind. I know it's stupid, but that's not something I want to do by myself."

Stede chewed on her words while he ate his

breakfast. He could understand her fears, but he couldn't wrap his mind around the size of Chase's ego. "Did you explain that to Chase?"

"No. He called me a few times, but I was too embarrassed to talk to him. Pretty soon, he moved on and started talking trash about me." She propped her arms on the bar and rested her head. "That's how I got the rep for being a tease and was essentially blacklisted. I can't say I blame him. I shouldn't have done what I did."

He stopped himself before he reached over to rub her back and offer her comfort. He balled his fists instead. "What about your friends? Your sorority sisters?"

"For a while, being seen with me was social suicide. It's gotten better over time, and when it's just us in the house, they're great, but things change if Chase is around. It's probably my fault for not confiding in them."

He knew a little about fair weather friends from his childhood. After his dad split and his mom took on extra jobs, he couldn't afford a gift for a classmate's birthday party. He had a crush on the girl and wanted to give her something, so he snuck into his mom's room, stole a bottle of perfume, and wrapped it in newspaper. Some of the kids laughed when the girl opened it because her mom pointed out that his mom might miss it in front of everyone. Things were different at school the next week.

"Embry, I can see you'd rather avoid conflict than stand up for yourself, but you need to know something. Chase has power over you because you gave it to him. You made yourself feel guilty over a choice you made to protect yourself. There's something very wrong with this picture."

Her jaw clenched as she stood. "Don't you think I know it's all my fault? I don't know how to fix it, besides trying to change my reputation."

"You could try standing up for yourself."

She took their plates and washed them before he could stop her. Judging by the force she dried them with, he would be better off not getting too close.

She folded the hand towel and placed it by the sink. "Can you please take me home?"

Chapter Seven

Embry was angry with herself for sharing her story with Stede. He was a guy. She should've known he'd have no sympathy for her.

On the motorcycle ride back to her car, which she'd driven to the bar in case she got left again, she tried to let go of the anger. His words hurt because they were true. Her sorority sisters should've supported her more, and she did need to stand up for herself, but she didn't know how.

When they got to the bar, she got off the bike and tried to figure out what to say. *Thank you for possibly saving me from date rape*. She shook her head and cut off that line of thought. It was too horrible to imagine.

"It's easier in jeans." She pointed to the bike.

"Give me your phone." He held out his hand.

She did and watched him program his number in. "Text me if you get into trouble. Find out Trent's last name and let me know. Stay away from him."

"Stop giving me orders. I'm not one of your freaking subordinates." She snatched her phone away and turned to go.

She didn't look back, but she knew he was still sitting there when she drove away. Tears filled her eyes and she got even angrier at herself for crying. She ground her teeth and gave herself a pep talk.

Stop being such a wimp. Pull up your bootstraps and act like the adult you want to be. Demand respect.

When she pulled up at the house, she took a deep breath before she went in.

Chanel was putting on makeup when she got to their room. "Ooh, someone stayed out all night. Who is he?"

Embry faked a smile as she grabbed clean clothes and a towel. "No one you know."

Keep 'em guessing was going to be her motto. While she got ready for the visits from potential pledges, she thought about how to get the respect of her sisters. The only way she could think of was to be honest.

They gathered downstairs a few minutes before they opened the doors. Their president gave a speech reminding everyone to smile and show their Eta Alpha spirit.

"I've got something to say." Embry stood and walked to where Brielle stood. "I'd have more spirit if I knew my sisters had my back. Two years is too long to suffer for what I did. I'm drawing a line in the sand. You're either my sister and my friend, or you're not. Don't be nice to me in private and ignore me in public."

"She's right." Brielle put her arm around Embry. "Chase is out of control."

"Hey," Chanel said. "That's my boyfriend you're talking about."

"Honey, if you think you're the only girl Chase is screwing, you're dumber than you look," Carol Anne's roommate said.

"Kelly," Carol Anne screeched. "You promised not to say anything."

"I'm tired of sitting back and letting Chase and his cronies control us," Kelly said.

Embry wanted to say something before someone started hair pulling. "Sisters, it's time we started respecting ourselves and each other."

"Amen, sister," Brielle said.

With the exception of Chanel, who sat pouting, the girls moved in for a group hug. Embry later embraced the knowledge her speech united the house and made them closer than they'd ever been.

It was a good day. They had a lot of visitors, sweet girls with wide eyes and big hopes for an awesome college experience. Embry truly hoped they'd get it and make wonderful memories to take with them when they entered the real world.

"Hey, Em." Brielle closed the distance between them. "I'm telling potential recruits to meet us on the patio at the pizza place later. We can eat, drink, whatever. The point is we're not going to Pete's Place because you-know-who will be there."

Embry released the mental breath she'd been holding. She felt bad about Pete losing the business, but she was so glad to have someone clearly on her side again.

* * *

Stede checked the schedule when he got to work Thursday evening. Embry wasn't on until Friday night, but Pete said she and her sisters came in most nights to hang out and meet up with some of the fraternity brothers. That night, the only one who came in was the one attached to Chase. She obviously didn't know he was getting serviced by other girls. Or at least that's what Stede thought right up until she yelled and poured a pitcher of beer on Chase's head.

The brothers cheered and laughed, but Chase shoved the table away and stood, causing his chair to tumble over, his face red as fire. Stede turned away to conceal his smile as Chase stomped down the hall to the bathroom.

A few minutes later, he came to the bar. "Hey, man, when's Embry working again?"

"Don't know."

"Trent said she ditched him last night. I was wondering if she went home with you."

"Trent who?"

"Stevens. New guy. Listen, I'm doubling the prize. I need you to work on her as soon as possible."

Stede raised an eyebrow. "Man, I can't see her until we work together."

"Forget it. I'll get someone else on it."

Stede didn't stop Chase when he walked away. Not having to get close to Embry was for the best since he'd pissed her off, not that he was taking bets or prizes for bedding a woman. Doing so was asinine and any man who was willing to do it needed a knot snatched in his ass.

On his next break, Stede called a buddy from school who worked for state law enforcement. He gave him the name of the guy he suspected of drugging Embry. He hoped she was safe and that she'd call him if she got in trouble. He considered calling GiGi to ask about her, but didn't want his grandmother to think anything was going on between them. He'd assured her he would stay away from all sorority girls.

On Friday night, Embry came in with smiles for everyone. There was something different about the way she carried herself. Her shoulders were back and her chin was lifted. Confidence looked damn good on her. She wasn't an island girl anymore. She was an island princess.

"Somebody must've gotten laid." Michelle put a pitcher of beer on her tray. "I've never seen her that happy."

His stomach knotted. He turned and mumbled a few choice words as he inserted a pour spout into a bottle with more force than the job required.

"Hey, Stede."

He faced Embry.

"I never thanked you for looking out for me the other night."

He propped a hand on the bar. "There's something I need to tell you."

"Let's move, Princess." Michelle nudged her. "It's Friday night and we're slammed."

"Talk later?" Embry asked as she backed away.

He nodded. Michelle had called it. They were slammed.

Then Chase and company came in and started harassing Embry.

Pete caught her at the bar. "You and Michelle switch sections. I'm about to have a come to Jesus meeting with that crew."

Michelle patted Embry's back and filled her in on her tables.

Stede was about to take his break, but wanted to make sure Pete didn't need him. He stood at the corner of the section and watched.

"Boys, I'm only going to say this once." Pete put his hands on the back of two of the guys' chairs. "You mess with my staff, you mess with me. If you can't use the manners your parents taught you, I'll be in touch with the Greek Council at the school. Now, you can stay. Drink. Eat. Have a good time. But if I have to come back over here, you're out. Banned. All of you."

Stede smiled as many of them sat up straighter and offered apologies. Chase played it smart, keeping his head down and his mouth shut.

The staff backed Embry up because she busted her tail to do her job and help everyone else. And, she didn't complain about anything, even the frat boys.

When things were under control, Stede stepped out back. The cook was having a smoke, so they made small talk.

The door opened and Embry came out. "Hey, fellas."

The cook offered her a cigarette, but she turned it down with a grin. "I'm trying to quit."

"So." The cook inhaled deeply. "What's his

name?"

"Whose name?" Embry asked.

"The one who put that smile on your face."

"A guy didn't put this smile on my face. I put it there myself."

The cook dipped his head and raised his eyebrows. "Really?"

"Not like that, gutter brain." Embry swatted him.

The door opened. "Orders in, Cookie Monster. Get in the kitchen before I chase you with a wooden spoon."

"Ooh, kinky." The cook dropped his cig and ground it with his shoe. "Michelle, you can chase me anytime, sweet thing."

"I lied, you know." Embry leaned against the wall next to Stede when they were alone. "I can't take all the credit for my smile. You're partly responsible."

"Oh?" He turned to face her, keeping his shoulder on the wall.

"I took your advice and talked to my sisters. I'm so happy. All I had to do was ask for what I wanted. It was amazing." She talked so fast it was hard to keep up, but he got the gist of what had happened.

"Good for you, but I can't share the glory. It was all you, Island Princess."

"Not you, too. Wait." She turned to face him and put her hand on his arm. "Did you just call me—"

The door swung open again. "Princess, there's a guy in here looking for you," Pete said.

She let go of Stede and moved to the door. "Wonder who that could be?"

"I need to tell you something." Stede took a step after her.

"I'm not done telling you stuff either. Can we talk later?"

He nodded.

When the door shut, he leaned his head against the brick wall for a moment. He needed to get back inside to see if it was the same guy who'd drugged her and intervene if necessary.

From his position behind the bar, Stede could see Embry and a different guy near the door. He was a baby-faced prep who might not realize tucking his polo in showed off the extra weight he carried in front. Stede wondered if he was one of Chase's recruits.

Then Stede got too busy slinging drinks to keep up with Embry, but the staff kept tabs on her and updated him with regularity. He shrugged and shook his head, trying to show disinterest, but he was actually glad gossip came with the territory.

Stede had a lull and took a moment to clean before last call. When the final round of orders came in, Trent dumped a drunken Chase on a stool at the bar. "Wait here, I'll be right back."

Stede wanted to follow to make sure Trent didn't bother Embry, but before Stede could get away, Chase called him.

"You hit that yet, Pirate Man?" His head fell onto his arms which rested on the bar.

"Sure." Stede rolled his eyes. "We had five minutes of nasty out by the dumpster earlier."

Chase made a snorting sound, which Stede soon realized was a snore.

"All right, bro, let's go." Trent slapped Chase on the back, and Chase picked up his head.

"Hey, man. You hit it yet?"

"Not yet. Give me time." Trent caught Chase when he nearly fell off the stool.

When the door had closed behind them, Stede noticed a cell phone on the bar where Chase had passed out. He stuck it in his back pocket, so he could wipe down the bar and made a mental note to put it in lost and found.

Chapter Eight

Embry sat on the trunk of her car, which was parked in front of the garage apartment where Stede lived. She hadn't gotten to talk to him after work because he'd been in Pete's office for a long time with the door closed. It became obvious she was waiting for someone after the third person asked what she was doing. She'd told them she was gonna thank Pete for helping with the fraternity boy situation, but she'd talk to him later.

When the headlight of Stede's Harley turned in and temporarily blinded her, she slid off the trunk and shielded her eyes. She reached back for the brown paper sack, and he stopped next to her.

"Is it okay that I'm here?" she asked. "If not, just tell me and I'll go."

"It's fine. Go on up. It's unlocked. I've got to put my baby to bed." He went to the garage door.

She laughed as she took the stairs. She found the light switch and took her brown sack all five steps into the kitchen. After a brief search, she found a baking sheet and went to work slicing cookie dough.

When Stede came in, he eyed the unused portion and grinned. "What you got there?"

"I don't know how to thank you, so I thought baking cookies might be a good start."

He dropped his backpack on the desk and took a seat at the bar. "Pass me the dough."

"You're not supposed to eat it raw. See," she pointed, "there's a warning right here on the label."

"The world's most ignored warning." He held his hand out. "Give it to me."

She leaned against the counter and watched him peel the plastic back and take a bite like it was a corn dog on a stick.

She shook her head. "Disgusting."

"You're the one who eats uncooked egg yolks. This is no different, and it tastes a heck of a lot better."

"Let me try a bite."

He held it close to his chest. "This is my present."

"One little tiny bite." She held up her thumb and forefinger to show how tiny.

He held it out and she took a small bite.

"Gosh, that's good."

"What made you so brave?"

She shrugged because she didn't want to tell him he was the one who'd motivated her to try new things. The motorcycle. Standing up for herself. She might have done the latter without him, but it would've taken longer. She wished she had the courage to try kissing him. He caught her staring at his mouth while he chewed cookie dough. Her face warmed and she turned away to check the oven.

Opening the oven door didn't help because a blast of hot air hit her in the face, and she jumped back and hit the edge of the counter. "Ow."

He was on his feet beside her. "You okay?"

She reached behind her to rub the spot on her low back where the edge of the counter got her. "Yeah. Probably nothing an aspirin won't fix."

"Let me see." He put his hands on her arms to turn her.

"It's fine." She tried to keep her black shirt tucked in while he untucked it.

"Embry, please."

She stopped resisting and her heart raced as he knelt and lifted her shirt. Her skin pricked with goose bumps when he grazed the spot lightly with his fingertips. Everything tightened inside when his lips pressed against her back.

"All better?"

She twisted and looked down at him, but her mouth was too dry to speak, so she nodded.

He stood next to her and the kitchen shrunk with him so big and close. "We should check those cookies."

She found her voice and made herself move. "Yeah." She used a spatula to move the cookies to a plate. "Chanel broke up with Chase."

"Who?" He poured two glasses of milk.

"My roomie. She found out Chase was cheating on her. And to make matters worse, he's got some guys trying to do me and get it on video."

"I was gonna warn you about that guy Trent. He was accused of date rape last year at his old school, but the charges were dropped."

"Huh?" Her heart pounded. She could've become his victim. "That's why he acted interested in me, the jerk." She followed Stede to the couch where he sat after he placed their milk on the coffee table. "Wait, is that why you wanted his last name? To check him out?"

He nodded as he bit into a cookie.

"Why didn't you just tell me?"

He swallowed. "You were mad at me."

"No, I wasn't. Not really. I was mad at me. I did get mad when you barked orders at me. I'm glad my dad wasn't in the Corps long enough to pick that up because my sisters and I would've never been born. Mom wouldn't have put up with it."

A slow smile spread across his gorgeous face. "Your dad's a Marine."

"Yeah, a jarhead like you. Oorah. Semper Fi. Yippee ki-yay and all that."

He laughed and leaned back. "We don't say yippee ki-yay. At least, not traditionally."

She leaned back too.

"You gonna make me eat these cookies by myself?"

"They're yours. You earned them by being my hero. Twice."

He held her gaze for a moment and heat flashed in his eyes. The kind that stoked the fire he'd already started in her.

He reached for a cookie and held it to her mouth. "You got injured in the line of duty. You deserve one of these cookies."

She bit her lip for a second before she opened her mouth and he put the cookie in. She sunk her teeth into the warm cookie and thought it would melt in her mouth before she could chew it. After she swallowed, he brought the cookie close to her lips again, but this time, he was holding it with his teeth. Something clenched deep inside.

She moved closer and opened her mouth taking as much of the cookie as she could to get to his lips. She pulled back just enough to see his blue eyes while they both chewed. They swallowed at the same time, and she pressed her mouth to his. He smelled like a man and tasted like chocolate chips. It was enough to throw her into the orgasmasphere the second his tongue brushed hers.

When he deepened the kiss, it took all her restraint not to crawl onto his lap. She'd been right. He knew how to kiss. She planned to stop him if his hands began to roam, but they didn't. One hand was on her face, and the heat from his palm made her skin sizzle. The only thing she knew about the other hand was it wasn't on her, which made her a little sad.

She ran her hand down his free arm and interlaced their fingers. When he squeezed her hand, she was lost. In the kiss. In the moment. In him. A familiar exhilaration coursed through her, not unlike the rush she got on his bike. Her inhibitions fell away and she wanted to be closer.

When she moved, he broke the kiss. It was shocking not to have the perfect feel of his lips against hers, and she blinked a few times to force herself out of the spell she'd fallen under.

"Why?" He breathed hard. "Did you kiss me?"

Her muddled brain had no excuse, so she surprised herself with her answer. "You had chocolate," she touched the corner of his mouth, "there."

He laughed and stood adjusting his jeans. "Excuse me."

When he closed the bathroom door, she fell back against the couch cushion, buried her face in brown plaid, and let out a little scream while she simultaneously kicked her feet in the air.

"Everything okay?"

She froze, feet still in the air before she slowly sat up and faced him with what little dignity she could muster. "Sugar high."

He grinned. "That's my excuse too."

Chapter Nine

Damn, if Stede didn't want to lay Embry down on his older than dirt sofa and see how far she'd let him go. The cookie kiss had frazzled his brain, and listening to the island princess's sexy laugh was not diminishing his desire. He needed a strategy, but couldn't decide which course of action to take.

"Stede, can I ask you something?" She reached for another cookie. "Do you think I'm a tease because I'm unwilling to help you with that?" She pointed to his crotch.

He should probably be embarrassed, but it was a natural thing, and with her, he had no control over it.

Before he could answer, she spoke again. "It's not really that I'm unwilling to help. I kinda, um, really want to help, but," she put her hand up, "one of my new rules is to respect myself and it would just be a little, um, hussy-like, in my opinion, if I helped you. I must sound like a complete idiot."

"No, you don't." He chanced getting near her again and sat down. "You sound like a smart woman who thinks through the consequences of her actions. You know who you are and what you want. I respect that."

"Really?" Her eyes widened. "I'm still figuring out who I want to be and what I want. Both have changed since I met you."

He tilted his head to the side. "How?"

"I always imagined there was a little cookie cutter mold of how things were supposed to be." She pointed to the plate. "I was going through the motions toward what I thought was my goal, but honestly, I was trying to live up to everyone's expectations of me without really figuring out what I wanted."

"And you think you know what you want now?"

"Yeah." She glanced down to his lap and then up to meet his eyes. "I want you."

He eased a throw pillow into his lap. "Not a good idea."

"I know you have a hundred reasons not to date me, but hear me out. I'm not asking for forever. In fact, I've decided I want to move out of South Carolina after I graduate next spring. I'm thinking D.C. With my art history degree, the Smithsonian is calling my name."

Stede shifted in his seat. He planned to move to D.C. after graduation too, but he had a couple years to go.

She continued. "I trust you and we can keep it secret if you want. In fact, I'd prefer it. Not that I'm ashamed of you. I'd be proud to step out with you, but I'd love to have some privacy, and not have my sisters hound me to tell them how good you are in bed."

"What about your '*In condoms, I don't trust*' motto?" he asked, since sex was on the table. He cut his eyes to the coffee table and had an entire fantasy about laying her down on it.

She bit her lip and squeezed her eyes closed. "I got on birth control the other day." She opened one eye to peek at him. "What? I wanted to turn my reputation around, and at the time, it seemed like a good plan. I figured I wouldn't panic if I had backup."

He couldn't argue. "Smart."

She exhaled and looked up. "Any other objections?"

He put his hand up. "Let me stop you right there."

"You can't tell me you're not interested. The proof is hiding behind that pillow." She pointed to his lap.

"I wasn't going to say I'm not interested, clearly I am." He lifted the pillow and replaced it. "I was going to say I didn't think you were my type until I started to get to know you a little. Now, I'm questioning what my type is."

She smiled and threw her arms around his neck. "Are you saying yes?"

He narrowed his eyes, not completely ignoring the little voice in his head telling him to proceed with caution. "Let's take it one day at a time and see how it goes."

She'd made him an offer no man could refuse. Sex with no long-term commitment. He was willing to bet she wanted exclusivity, but so did he. If he saw Trent or any of the brothers breathing her air, he might be tempted to toss a grenade in their front door. He wouldn't actually do it, but the mental image gave him a great deal of satisfaction.

He put his hand on her cheek and ran his thumb across her lips, which parted in response. The breath that escaped smelled of chocolate chip delight, and he covered her mouth with his so he could have more.

* * *

They fell asleep kissing on the couch, lying on their sides facing each other. When Embry opened her eyes, her face was an inch from his, and their bodies were front to front with his solid arms around her.

Her lower belly clenched, reminding her how much she wanted him and how hard it had been to keep their clothes on the night before. His hard body pressed against her softer one, and they fit together perfectly.

Stede's hand on the small of her back pulled her closer, and she arched into him. If he was as good at sex as he was at kissing, she was in for a treat. With the guys she'd slept with before, she'd never really let herself go enough to enjoy it.

His eyes opened and he blinked once before a slow grin spread across his face. Waking up to him every morning was a woman's dream come true. The flutter in her chest served as a warning. She'd offered him no strings, and she intended to follow through, even if her heart tried to get caught up in the deal.

"Mornin', Island Princess."

Her smile grew bigger. She brushed the back of her fingers across his stubble-covered cheek. "Mornin', Gentleman Pirate."

He rolled her to her back and gave her a quick kiss before he got up. "I gotta get to my toothbrush before you try cleaning the toilet with it again."

She laughed and sat up. It was her day off from work and sorority life. Starting Monday, things would get hectic, but today was hers and she hoped Stede had some time to spend hanging out. He wasn't on the work schedule, but that didn't mean he didn't have schoolwork or errands to run.

The bathroom door opened. "Do you need to get in here before I jump in the shower?"

"Yeah, I'll be quick." She brushed past him.

When she came out, he waited with clothes in his hand. "I've got to open for Pete in an hour."

"Oh, okay. I'll get out of your hair." She hesitated, trying to hide her disappointment. "Unless…can I make you an egg sandwich before I go?"

He stretched an arm toward the kitchen area. "Be my guest, but no runny yolks for me."

"I know, I know. Do you want the mayo?"

"Yeah, it was good that way." He closed the door and the shower came on.

While she scrambled eggs for them both, she couldn't keep her mind from imagining what he looked like in the shower. Naked and muscled and wet. She was so hot for him she believed she could boil eggs by holding them in her hands.

Her mind still occupied, she didn't hear him come out of the bathroom and walk up behind her. Her heart jumped in her chest when he pressed her into the counter.

His lips grazed her ear when he spoke. "You wanna ride with me later."

I wanna ride you *later.* "Heck, yeah. When do you want me?" She turned to face him and from the heat in his eyes, her question got the desired result. "To come back, I mean."

Chapter Ten

Stede tried to conceal his good mood when Pete got into work sooner than expected.

"Thanks for helping me out this morning," Pete said. "If you want off tomorrow, I'll cover your shift."

"Nah, I'll come in." He'd already checked the schedule to see that Embry was working lunch, too.

"Good man." Pete slapped him on the back. "Now get out of here and enjoy your Saturday."

He was disappointed Embry wasn't at his apartment when he arrived. He looked up at the graying sky and readjusted the ride he'd planned. He'd wanted to take her around the big lake, but the weather was to the south, which meant they should head north to the National Forest. There was a smaller lake there, but it would still be a nice spot to picnic.

He made sandwiches and almost had his backpack filled when she came in.

"Sorry I'm late." She set a grocery sack on the bar. "I got water and peanut butter crackers so we'd have something to snack on later."

He grinned because he'd intended to surprise her with the picnic. "You're the one wearing the backpack, so give it here. Let's load it down."

He zipped and lifted the pack, hoping it wouldn't be too heavy for her. It'd be much lighter on the way back. He double checked the small outer zipper to be sure he hadn't forgotten the most important thing, just in case. The shiny foil package reflected the overhead light, and he closed it quickly. "You ready?"

"Almost." She walked right to him, stood on her tiptoes and planted a kiss on his lips. "Now, I'm ready."

He helped her get her helmet straps adjusted and buckled before he put his on. While she slipped her arms in the backpack straps, he got on the bike and cranked her up. The rumble vibrated through him, making every cell of his body feel alive. The only thing that made it better was when she slid on and pressed the front of her body against his back.

The road sped past as they made their way north. The wind in his face and the woman at his back sent a rush of elation through his soul.

He found a secluded spot to park his bike, and they hiked to the water's edge. He spread a red and white checkered blanket on the untouched shoreline.

When his landlady had heard the word *picnic*, she said she had just the thing. She'd offered him a wicker basket too. He smiled at the stories she'd told him about picnics she and her husband had shared when they were courting.

Embry, who had removed her shoes to test the water, turned to him. "Hey—oh, my God." She let out a little scream and ran and jumped into his arms, wrapping her legs around him. "You planned all this? If you keep this up, I might…"

"Might what?"

"Nothing." She unwrapped her legs and put her feet on the ground, but he didn't let go of her.

"Finish your sentence. You've got this new brave thing going on. Don't turn into a bahk-bahk." He released her and flapped his arms like a chicken.

"I'm not afraid." She put her hands on her hips. "I just don't want to scare you."

"How could a little island princess scare a big, bad pirate like me?"

Her smile revealed those pearly whites and full pink lips. He kissed her before she could answer. Then he motioned for her to sit so they could eat. It was early afternoon and neither of them had eaten since the egg sandwiches that morning. Their feast consisted of peanut butter and jelly sandwiches, peanut butter crackers, Cheez-its, and bottled water.

"These carbs are gonna stick to my butt." Embry opened her water and took a swig to chase down her last cracker.

"Come here to me." He pulled her onto her knees and laid her across his lap. He swatted her butt. "I'm gonna spank you every time you say something about your weight. Your body is just fine. Be brave."

She laughed, got back to her knees and gave

him a quick kiss. "I'm not sure how I feel about the kinky stuff. The spankings will probably be fine as long as I don't have to call you *Sir*."

His body reacted to her words, and he hadn't thought he was into the kinky stuff either. "Look what you did."

"Does it hurt if you don't, you know, release?"

He chuckled. "It depends. If I get close and stop, it can be uncomfortable."

"Oh, good. I mean, not good, but I was worried, you know, about you, from last night…and right now."

"Do you have any more extremely personal questions about sex organs for me?" He leaned back on his elbows.

"Do you like big boobs or are small ones okay?"

His head fell back as he laughed. "I'm a man. I'll take 'em any way they come."

"The reason I ask is…" She hesitated and looked down.

"You're afraid I won't like yours. Let me reassure you, you're perfect the way you are."

"But I wear padded bras."

He shrugged. "So?"

"You don't think I'm a fraud."

"I might have to spank you again."

Thunder rumbled in the distance and wind rustled the trees.

"We better move." He gathered up their trash and stuffed it in the backpack along with the blanket.

* * *

Embry had a hard time with the helmet strap again. His eyes smiled and his hands were gentle as he fixed it for her. Then he patted her head before he threw his leg over his bike. Sexy wasn't meaningful enough to convey how masculine and tender he was at the same time. The vibration of the bike related the need growing inside her.

As fat drops of rain began to fall, she spotted a patch of red through the thick growth of trees ahead and pointed. Stede slowed and turned onto the overgrown dirt path leading into the woods. There was a small wooden building in a clearing, and the faded red paint was peeling.

He stopped the bike, and without discussion, she jogged over to check the door. It opened to an empty space no larger than Stede's apartment. It had a dirt floor and probably had housed outdoor equipment or maybe even animals. She motioned for him to come in.

He rolled the bike in and got off, removing his helmet. "I guess we can wait out the storm and finish our picnic."

"We weren't finished?" She removed the backpack from her shoulders.

He took it from her. "I was saving the surprise for last."

He pulled out the red and white blanket and together they spread it in the center of the space. He reached into the pack and came out with a bottle of Champagne.

"No dang wonder that thing was so heavy." She joked to cover up the rhythmic beating of her heart, which was increasing every second.

He placed two plastic flutes and a container of strawberries on the center of the blanket next to LED tea light candles. The sky outside grew darker as the storm closed in. The scene was perfect. It had seduction written all over it, but it was exactly what she wanted.

She squealed when the cork popped, and they tapped their cups together before they sipped the bubbly drink. It tickled all the way down.

"I don't know what to do with these strawberries." He gestured to the container.

"You've never done this before?"

"No. My mom always said it'd be her dream come true for a man to take her on a picnic with Champagne and strawberries." He shrugged with a strawberry in one hand and his glass in the other. "She never said what to do with these two things."

"I've never tried it before either." She moved closer to him on her knees and took a strawberry. "But, I think you're supposed to bite into the strawberry and sip the Champagne right after."

She held her strawberry to his lips while he opened for a small bite. Then he sipped.

"Um, it's good. Sweet and a little creamy."

"Let me taste." She held still and he put his strawberry to her lips, but she shook her head. "Let me taste you."

His lips were on hers before she could take another breath and delicious landed in the center of her chest as a wildfire spread to every limb. A little breeze blew through the broken window, but it did nothing to cool her down.

She reached for the bottom of her shirt. Having

to get it off, she broke the kiss and yanked it over her head. Stede stared at her chest and she remembered his words. *Be brave*. Without another thought, she unhooked her bra and dropped it next to her shirt. She watched his reaction.

A small grin formed even as desire crossed his features. "Perfect."

She reached for his waistband and took his T-shirt in both hands. He raised his arms and she lifted his shirt over his head. He caught her arms at the top, tossed the shirt, and clasped her hands in each of his. She left his eyes and took a moment to see what she already knew. He had a magazine cover-ready body to go with his face.

He closed the space between them until her chest was against his as he lowered their arms. His muscles moved against her, causing a spasm between her thighs as she anticipated what would follow.

They spent a while exploring each other from the waist up until she was more than ready to get the rest of their clothes off. When she reached for his jeans clasp, he held up a finger to stop her.

Reaching into the backpack, he produced condoms. "For when you're ready." He put them on the blanket.

She didn't hesitate, but again reached for his button. "This might be easier if we stand."

They did and she slowly lowered his jeans, bending down until he stepped out of them. She wasn't really surprised he hadn't bothered with underwear. It was just one more thing to have to remove. She stood and took a step back to admire him. He was everything she hoped for and more. Maybe more than she could handle, but she'd do her best.

Another spasm.

He bit his lower lip and gave her the sexiest come hither finger gesture she'd ever seen. She might completely spaz out before her pants came off. Instead of walking into his arms again, she reached for the button on her jeans. For some reason, removing her own clothes and his was her way of making a statement. She was going after what she wanted. She slipped her thumbs inside her panties and removed both garments with a slow shimmy of her hips.

He groaned.

She kicked the clothes aside and walked to him. She ran her fingertips over the eagle, globe, and anchor tattoo on his chest, and goose bumps rose on his flesh despite the heat in their rainy day hideaway.

He scooped her in his arms, went to his knees, and lowered her onto the blanket before he knelt over her, kissing his way down her body.

It was time to explore new territory. She only thought he was a great kisser with his mouth on hers. She'd never been kissed down there before.

She let go and rode the wave of pleasure until she wasn't sure if the lightning flashed in her mind or outside their love shack.

The triumphant look on his face was not lost on her, and she wanted a victory of her own. "My turn."

She'd never liked doing it much before, but

Stede had been unselfish and unrestrained. She wanted to make him feel good and make it so he'd never forget her.

He rolled onto his back, and she started with his lips, kissing her way down. He propped up on his elbows to watch her at first, but soon he dropped to his back and rocked his hips while he gripped fistfuls of the picnic blanket. She could get used to the rush of power flooding through her as she made him feel so intensely.

"God bless America." Every muscle clenched when he came, then relaxed as he lay still.

She rested her head on his thick muscled thigh. "Are you always so patriotic?"

He leaned up on his elbows and bit his lip in that sexy way she loved. She was in trouble. There was no way she'd be able to walk away from him when the time came.

Chapter Eleven

Stede kept his eyes fixed on Embry. She looked damn good climbing up his body on her hands and knees before stretching out by his side.

"I guess we have to wait a little while now." Her fingertip left a line of raised goose flesh as she trailed it along his chest.

He rolled her over so he was on top. "I guess we'll have to find something to pass the time." He kissed her neck. "It won't be long."

"We have snacks." Her smile lit up the dim space.

He took a strawberry and starting at her jawline, used it to draw on her flawless skin. His mouth followed and when he reached her belly button, a stroke of genius hit him.

He reached for the Champagne bottle and poured a little across her smooth flat stomach. He bit the strawberry and licked her skin. Her back arched and time was up. He was ready.

He debated for a moment whether to let her finish what she'd started and be in charge, or if it was his turn to claim her the way he'd been dying to do since the first time she got on his bike.

He knew her history and didn't want her to panic so he took his time. He positioned himself between her legs and poured more Champagne, which he promptly lapped up with his tongue. She writhed beneath his kiss, and she was as ready as him.

"S-Stede."

He looked up into her big dark eyes. "Yes?"

"I want you." She held up a small foil packet. "Now."

"Whatever my island princess wants, she gets." He crawled up, kissing as much of her flesh as he could along the way.

He started to take the condom from her, but stopped. "You should do the honors."

She blushed and bit her lower lip. "Okay."

He held himself up over her while she opened the package and tried to put it on.

"It doesn't work." Her voice was shaky.

He sat up on his knees. "Sure it does." He took her hands and saw that it was the wrong way. "Turn it around, and roll it on." At the last moment, he said, "Please."

She did, and when he was fully covered, she smiled. "That's harder than it looks."

"You have no idea."

She laughed. "I meant getting it on, but…" she hesitated, "you too."

Heat flashed in her eyes, and he bent to kiss

her. The slight delay might have taken some of her courage, and he was determined to take his time, to be sure she was ready. The way she returned his kiss left little doubt.

He moved between her thighs and waited for her. Her legs wrapped around him, and she lifted her hips as she reached down with one hand to grip him.

She guided him home, and he held there. It had been a while for her; he needed to go slow. His heartbeat was louder than the thunder, and his blood rushed faster than the heavy rain falling on the tin roof.

"Please." Her voice was a whisper as she arched her back up and down again, thrusting her hips higher and allowing him to sink a little deeper.

Little by little, he settled in, and before he was all the way there, she rocked her hips and cried out his name. He plunged deeper, and when it was over, he'd given her everything, including his heart.

As they lay in each other's arms in the wake of the storm raging outside, the smell of their lovemaking lingered in the humid air. As long as he lived, he'd never go through another thunder shower and not remember his island princess.

It was dark when the rain stopped, and he stepped into his jeans and boots to walk outside and check the sky. The clouds had moved off to the northeast. In the southern sky, stars dotted the midnight blue velvet. A hint of fall sent a chill rushing along his skin. The sensation increased as Embry's arms encircled him from behind.

"You ready to go, Princess?"

"No, but I guess we should get back, in case more bad weather comes." Her lips pressed onto his shoulder.

He shivered and turned to put his arms around her. She fit like no other woman before her ever had.

Or would again.

* * *

On the ride back to Stede's place, Embry hugged him close and rested her cheek against his back. The fresh smell of earth after a cleansing rain filled her lungs. Like the rain, Stede's love had washed over her, removed every fear, and given her every pleasure.

She'd never forget their little shack and when they'd laid together afterward, there was no awkwardness like she'd experienced after previous sexual encounters. She wondered if she should even count the others because she'd never felt what she should for them.

Love.

She pushed the word away, reminding herself of her offer. She could feel it; she just couldn't let him know it.

She got off the bike and walked into the garage with him, giving him her helmet. "I guess I should go."

He put the helmet on a bench and turned, taking her hands. "I wish you'd stay."

Her heart lifted. "Really?"

He answered her with a kiss before he scooped her into his arms and carried her up the stairs to his apartment. He set her down inside the door and turned on the light. "How about a shower? I didn't think about how sticky that Champagne might be when I soaked you with it."

She laughed as her cheeks warmed. "I'm pretty sure you licked most of it off, but I'm not opposed to a shower, if you'll join me."

He was already stripping off his T-shirt, and she grinned as she backed up toward the bathroom.

He washed her first, and she dropped her head back as her soapy body tightened before release. Thankfully, he held her up when her legs almost refused to support her.

When she washed him, she spent a while on his well-muscled butt. "How does a body get a booty like this?"

He turned to face her, and her hands moved to his chest. "Argh. Ye can have me chest, but leave me booty alone."

She doubled over with laughter. When she was done, she reached around and groped his butt with soapy hands. "I want both."

"To answer your question, I thank running."

"I guess you have to do a lot of that in the Marines?"

"Yeah, but I ran high school track before that. Mom told me to pick a sport that wasn't too expensive."

She thought about the opportunities her parents had offered her to try every activity and pick one. Now that money was something she had to work for, she couldn't imagine buying a tennis racket for a kid only to have him to decide he didn't like the sport. Which was what she'd done.

She splashed clean water on Stede's body to rinse the soap off. "I only run if I'm being chased."

He turned off the water and looked over his shoulder. "I'll give you a head start."

She screamed and took off, which is how she ended up getting dried off by his sheets as he took her to the mattress.

When they lay there later, she took a moment to be thankful for him. He held on to her as much as she needed him to. She was afraid to act too clingy, but he didn't seem to care about appearances.

During lovemaking, he'd whispered her name and told her she was beautiful. The memory of his voice in her ear made her chest tighten.

"I hope you don't mind that I asked you to stay." He played with a strand of her hair. "I don't know how long I have you, and I don't want to waste a minute."

She sighed. If she didn't have sorority commitments, she'd have more time.

He leaned up to look at her. "Hey." He brushed her cheek with his fingers. "Don't stress. I'll take whatever you can give me."

"Even if all I have is a late night after work? Or after a function?"

"The door will be open for you."

"But…what if you have other company?" She gritted her teeth.

"Do you actually think I'd be able to look at another woman after you?"

She smiled in her heart at the same time it showed on her face. She drew on his chest with her finger, but made herself stop when she realized she was drawing hearts. Hopefully, he hadn't noticed.

"Just don't go flaunting any frat boys in front of me, and I won't have to break their faces."

"I wouldn't do that, Stede."

He squeezed her closer and kissed her forehead. "Sweet dreams, my island princess."

"Sweet dreams, my gentleman pirate. You definitely got the booty." She nuzzled her face into chest as he shook with laughter.

Chapter Twelve

Stede kept his eyes down as he worked, certain if he looked at Embry, everyone would see through him. He wasn't sure how the little princess had stolen his heart in such a short time, but if anyone found out, he'd catch hell for breaking his own rules. He was especially guarded around Michelle, since she liked to gossip.

He was putting her drink orders on the server's station at the end of the bar when she approached. "Did you hear what happened last night?"

Stede shook his head.

"That kid, Chase, came in here yelling and tearing shit up. Said he lost his cell phone and there was important stuff on it."

Oops. Stede didn't say it out loud. He knew exactly where the punk's cell phone was. "Is that why there are broken chairs in the dumpster out back?"

"Yeah. After Pete checked lost and found and

gave Chase the bad news, the kid picked up a chair and slammed it down and then another. Pete called the cops on him." She hefted her drink tray and walked away.

Stede thought about his choices. He'd forgotten about the damn thing. He could put it near the trash can in the men's room and let someone find it and turn it in. Or, Stede could just chunk it in the dumpster and be done with it. He hated being deceitful, and he was sure the kid would have a new cell in a day or so.

Michelle returned a few minutes later. "I asked the kid if he had that *find my phone* thing before the cops hauled him off."

Stede's body tensed. "And?"

"He said it didn't work if the battery was dead."

Stede's breath rushed out. He had images of Chase trashing his apartment to find the phone. "Did he say what the important stuff was?"

"Probably naked pictures of half the sorority girls." Michelle winked. "On the bright side, he won't be back in here to harass the princess."

Stede was glad about that, but he was distracted by what might be on the phone. He had turned the phone off and never checked its contents. To protect Embry, he was willing to chance it. He was confident he wouldn't find naked pictures of her, but after the wager Chase tried to make with him, he bet there was something damaging to someone's reputation on there. He should probably turn it over to the cops.

"Did you hear?"

He looked up to see a smiling Embry at the server's station. His smile was automatic, but he dialed it down a notch when she blushed.

"I heard."

"It took all my willpower not to do the happy dance when Michelle told me."

He propped his elbows on the bar and cleared his throat. "You can show me how that dance goes later."

"Be happy to."

"Happy to what?" Michelle plopped a tray on the bar.

"Deliver some flowers to my grandmother for me later this week." Stede straightened. "I'd do it myself, but Embry told me rush is about to be in full swing and the last place I want to be—"

"Is in a house full of hormonal women," Michelle finished with a laugh.

"Exactly." Stede crossed his eyes before he turned his back to the ladies. He bent to restock the paper goods, but could still hear them.

"Would you look at that ass?" Michelle said. "I bet you could bounce a quarter off of it. I'd like to get my hands on it and see."

"Yeah. He must work out," Embry said, making him smile like a fool.

* * *

The next week was slammed with rush activities, most of which Embry managed to attend between working and sneaking off to see her pirate.

One night, when they'd lay tangled in his sheets, she propped up on an elbow. "I like being your booty call."

He'd rolled her over and looked into her eyes. "You're so much more to me than that, Princess."

Her heart had lurched and thumped, and she'd almost blurted out she loved him. She'd changed her entire notion of the kind of man she wanted to settle down with some day.

There was one man, and he treated her like his princess.

After membership bids were given out, Embry hurried back to her room at the house to change for the evening shift. Stede would be working, and even though they kept it from everyone, she still enjoyed stealing glances at him.

When she was tying her shoes, Chanel came in. "All right. Who is it?"

"Who is it what?"

"Your secret lover. What do you think? That we don't all know you're sneaking in at sunrise?"

Embry tried not to smile. "Leave it alone."

Chanel put her hands on her hips. "Why?"

"Because it's none of your business." She'd always wanted to say that, but never had the courage.

Chanel gasped. "You used to be so sweet."

"I used to be a doormat, but those days are over." Embry brushed past her on the way out.

"It might be a trick, you know."

Embry turned back. "What might be a trick?"

"The guy. He might be one of the one's Chase recruited to get to you."

Embry smiled and shook her head. "Not this one. No way. No how."

* * *

Embry beat Stede to his apartment after work that night and let herself in. He'd mentioned there was a DVD they could watch, so she walked over to his desk to see what he'd chosen. She smiled at the totally testosterone filled selection—*Fast and Furious*.

She placed the movie on his laptop and noticed a cell phone. It was odd because he had his with him. He'd texted her he was stopping for gas and snacks when he left Pete's Place. Her mind immediately went to Chase and the phone he'd lost.

She shook her head and returned it to the desk. There was no reason for Stede to have Chase's phone.

The door opened behind her, and she rushed into his arms.

He picked her up to kiss her before he set her back on her feet. "I got you something."

"What?" She locked her hands behind his neck.

He opened the plastic bag in his hand and pulled out a black T-shirt. It had a white skull and crossbones under the words *Pirate Girl*.

She laughed and took it from him. "It's perfect. I love it, almost as much as I…"

He tilted his head and cut his eyes. "Almost as much as what?"

"As I." Her voice was shaky so she swallowed. "I love you."

She couldn't believe she'd actually said it. If he didn't run screaming, she'd take it as a good sign.

His hands were on her hips, and one of them slid around to the small of her back and pulled her tight against him. "I think gentleman pirates and island princesses are meant to be together, don't you?"

It wasn't *I love you too*, but she'd take it, and when his lips captured hers, he was saying it without words.

* * *

The next evening, Embry didn't have to work and she'd vowed to herself and Stede that she would give running a try. She put on her new pirate T-shirt, shorts, and sneakers and set out for a short jog around campus. She exited the Greek Village when she saw Chase running toward her on the other side of the street. She kept her chin up and eyes forward, but she wasn't too surprised when he crossed over and joined her.

"Looking good, Tease-Me-Embry." He ran backward beside her. "I especially like the shirt. Does that mean a certain pirate is hitting that?"

"No, it doesn't. Go away." She picked up the pace, and he turned around and stayed with her.

"Where'd you get the shirt?"

"From the getting place."

"Yeah, tell the pirate to come see me and bring the video. I'll pay him what I owe him."

Embry tripped over her own feet and went down hard onto the concrete.

Chase laughed and didn't offer to help her up. "If I hadn't lost my phone, I'd play the evidence for you."

He was still laughing when he jogged off.

Embry managed to get to her feet. Her ears were ringing, and she stumbled a little. Looking down, she noticed the blood on her palms and streaming down the front of her legs from her knees. She limped back toward her house, all the while Chase's words played in her head. He couldn't have been talking about Stede. It didn't make sense, but the shirt, the phone, Chanel's warning.

"No," she said aloud. "He wouldn't."

She knew what she had to do to prove Stede wasn't involved. She made it back to the house, got into her car, and drove to his apartment.

Chapter Thirteen

Stede smiled when he pulled up and saw Embry's car. He took the stairs two at a time. It'd been a slow night at work, so Pete had sent him home early. He texted Embry to let her know, but when she didn't respond, he assumed she was busy with sorority stuff.

He opened the door and saw her on the couch. Normally, she jumped in his arms when he came in, but now she sat looking off into space.

That's when he saw the blood.

"Oh, my God." He pushed the coffee table aside and went to his knees in front of her. "Em, what happened?"

She narrowed her eyes when she looked at him. "Where is it?"

"Where's what, Princess? What happened to you?" He went to the kitchen and wet some paper towels.

"The video." She spoke through clenched teeth.

She must be in pain.

He bent in front of her and placed a paper towel on her knee. "I didn't rent a video today."

She sucked in air when he wiped down the front of her leg. That was when he saw it in her hand. Chase's phone. The one Stede had hung onto because he didn't want to return it after he'd discovered what was on it. Information Embry now knew judging by the hate in her eyes.

"Just delete the video. Right now. And I'll go." Tears welled in her eyes.

"Oh, baby, no. You misunderstood. There's no video."

She kicked him in the balls, and he curled into the fetal position as he toppled over onto his side.

She stood and limped to the door. "If I ever see or hear about a video, I will have you arrested. Don't call me or look at me ever again."

"Embry." He coughed between gasps for air. "It's not what you think."

It was too late. She slammed the door behind her. He struggled to get to his knees and go after her, but a cramp in his groin had him back on the floor. She'd probably caused permanent damage, but it was nowhere near the damage he'd done by not telling her about Chase from the start.

Eventually, he crawled to the freezer and pulled out a bag of peas. He laid on the kitchen floor and groaned at the pressure of the frozen food on his groin. He'd rather focus on the physical discomfort than the pain in his chest at losing her.

The audio recording Chase had made of their conversation was incriminating without a doubt.

Stede had to make Embry understand he was doing it for her. Every explanation he rehearsed in his mind sounded like an excuse. He'd made a huge mistake. One she might not forgive. Maybe he should let her go since she wasn't what he'd wanted in his life. He had been fine before her. He had school and work. Except, she was exactly what he needed. He was head over in heels in love with the woman. And letting her go, would mean letting Chase win.

Stede wasn't going to let that happen.

* * *

Embry showered, cleaned her wounds, and crawled into bed. When her alarm went off the next day, she called Pete to tell him she couldn't come in for a few days. She almost quit so she'd never have to see the lying pirate again, but that went against her new attitude. She intended to stand strong in the face of adversity. Besides, no one knew about Stede, yet. Except maybe Chase. If he got the proof he wanted, the whole world would know. When that happened, she was gonna take them both down. In fact, she debated calling the cops before she pulled the covers over her head and went back to sleep.

She'd been dumb to wear the T-shirt in public. It was like advertising she'd done it with a guy named after a pirate. Chase might be a total scumbag, but he wasn't stupid.

The only time Embry got out of bed was to pee, and it hurt so much to move she decided to hold it as long as possible. Chanel came in and out several times during the day, but she knew Embry had taken a nasty fall and was letting her rest.

Embry wished she had a private place to rest and lick her wounds. Stede's apartment would be ideal, but she could never go back there. She'd been a fool, offering herself to him. He hadn't even had to work for his money because she'd trusted him.

Her heart clenched and pain shot through her chest. She used the undamaged side of her hand to rub the spot, hoping it would go away. She'd given Stede so much more than her body, and his betrayal threatened to break her.

* * *

Late in the day, GiGi came in with a tray of food. "I heated some soup. How are you feeling, honey?"

Embry's eyes filled with tears. She couldn't know her own grandson was so terrible.

"If you're still hurting that bad, maybe I should take you to the doctor. Or, call your parents."

"No." Embry sniffed. "I'll be better in a day or two. Thanks for the soup."

GiGi pulled the stool over from the dressing table and sat next to the bed. "Are you sure you fell on your own? If someone did this to you, you can tell me."

Embry wanted to tell someone about her problems, but not GiGi. She thought her grandson was a hero. Embry had thought it once, too. She didn't have it in her to break GiGi's heart, so she didn't.

"I was just clumsy. Thought I could make it as a runner to keep my weight down, but clearly I need a new form of cardio."

"Did you know my Stede is a runner?"

Embry's breath caught in her throat at hearing his name. "No, ma'am."

"He ran on a team and they held the state record for a few years. Fast." GiGi smiled with pride. "If you want to give it another try, I bet he'll help you."

"That's okay. I think I'm done with the sport of running."

There was a knock at the door. GiGi opened it to Stede.

He walked past his grandmother and straight to Embry's bedside.

Her temper flared and she ground her teeth. "What are you doing here?"

"Yes, Stede. Why are you here? You shouldn't be in my girls' room." GiGi moved around to the other side of the bed.

He ignored GiGi. "Pete said you called in sick. I want to know what happened to you."

Embry blinked and warm tears fell down her face.

"She had a fall, Stede. Poor thing is all skinned up."

"Where were you? Were you pushed?" He sat on the edge of her bed.

The lump in her throat prevented her from answering, so she shook her head before she buried her face in her hands. "Go away."

"You should go, Stede. Poor thing is so upset."

"I'm not going anywhere." He slid closer and wrapped his arms around her.

He smelled so good. She wanted to bury her head in his chest and cry, until she remembered she hated him. She balled up her fists, but it hurt her palms, so she kept her hands open and beat on him with the fleshy part on the sides.

"Go away, liar. Go away." She choked and sobbed, but he held on to her.

Chapter Fourteen

"I'm never letting you go. I'm in love with you." Stede stroked her head.

"What?" GiGi asked.

"I'm sorry, GiGi. I know I promised. I tried *not* to fall for her, but I wanted to protect her from Chase and not falling for her was impossible." He turned his attention to Embry and braced her head with his hands. "You hear me? I know how that recording sounded to you."

She sobbed. "You lied. I trusted you."

"I know. But I didn't get close to you to trick you. After the night Trent drugged you, I thought I could keep you safe and away from the other guys, if I broke my rules and my promises."

"What other guys?" Her breath hitched.

"Did you listen to the entire recording? After I told him we had a deal, thinking that was all it would take, he told me I wasn't the only one after you."

"So you admit it, you were after me? To get a hundred stupid dollars." She shoved him.

"No, Embry. I didn't really take the bet; I only wanted Chase to think I did. Aren't you listening to me? I would never do what he asked me to do to a woman."

"I don't know what's going on," GiGi said. "But Stede wouldn't hurt anyone, especially not for money."

"Chase said…" Embry stopped and squeezed her eyes shut. "You tricked me."

Stede let out a growl and pulled away from her. "Yeah, Embry, go ahead and believe the guy who's made your life hell for two years over me."

"Now, Stede, you watch your tone young man." GiGi sat on the other side of the bed. "You know how to speak to a lady."

He ran his hand through his hair. "I know, but…" He sighed. "Please believe me."

"I…I want to go to the police." Embry rubbed her eyes. "I'm tired of Chase ruining my life."

The tension drained from his shoulders, and he pulled her into his arms. "Already done. I turned the phone in first thing this morning and filed a complaint. According to what's on that phone, Chase has been blackmailing and harassing a lot of people."

"Really?" Her puffy red eyes widened.

"Yeah. The officer asked me to bring you down so you can file a complaint, too." He brushed her hair back. "If that's what you want."

Embry hiccupped. "He laughed. I fell and hurt myself, and Chase stood there and laughed at me."

"That son-of-a—"

"Stede, watch your mouth." GiGi crossed her arms over her chest. "And as for that no good boy, I ought to bend him over my knee and beat the tar out of him."

Embry giggled and rested her head on Stede's shoulder. "I wish you would."

The door flew open and Chanel danced in. "Did you hear? Chase got arrested for extortion."

"That was fast," Stede said.

Sounds of cheering came from the floor below.

"Will you take me downstairs?" Embry put her arms around his neck.

GiGi pulled the covers down, exposing Embry's injuries.

"That bastard better be glad he's in jail, or I'd give him bruises to match yours and worse."

GiGi narrowed her eyes. "Stede Bennett, have you forgotten what soap tastes like?"

Embry laughed as he picked her up. She was in his arms, exactly where she belonged.

* * *

Embry felt like Scarlet O'Hara, except she was getting carried down the stairs, instead of up them. Her body still ached, but her heart was lighter. Stede was trying to save her. He'd been saving her since the first day they met.

He placed her on the sofa and sat next to her, holding her hand while her sisters told tales of Chase's sometimes criminal and always reprehensible behavior. Several of them admitted to giving sexual favors, so he wouldn't reveal something shameful they'd wanted kept secret.

They shared. They cried. They cheered.

Embry had no idea he'd made other people as miserable as he'd made her. Worse even. The day she'd drawn the line in the sand with her sisters they'd been glad someone was willing to begin standing up to him. They'd all been empowered by her about face.

She turned her head to look at Stede. "We have this man to thank. He believed in me. It made me feel like I could do anything, including change my situation with regard to Chase."

Stede put his arm around her and hugged her to his side. "I love you."

"Aww," chorused in the room.

"Where can I get me one of those?" someone asked.

Embry kissed him and then rested her head on his shoulder. "This one's mine, but there are a few good ones out there. Don't ever let them treat you like anything less than a princess."

He squeezed her shoulder.

"I found a good one," Brielle said. "I've been secretly seeing Mark. Chase had something on him, too. His cousin, Griffin, pledged Tri Mu because Mark didn't want him influenced by Chase."

"The cousin's cute. Maybe I'll ask him out," another sister said.

"I have his number," Embry said.

Stede tensed beside her, and she patted his leg. "He asked me out, and I told him I'd think about it. When I saw him a few days ago and told him I was seeing someone, he told me I could share his number if I knew any nice girls."

A cacophony of voices rose.

"Dibs."

"Mine."

"I want it."

Stede laughed. "That poor boy has no idea what he's gotten himself into."

"What about you? Do you know what you've gotten yourself into?" She smirked.

"Yes, I do." He stretched his free arm out in front of him. "I see my future. A long, happy life with a beautiful island princess."

"Can we live together for a while before we get married? I want to freak my parents out."

"Anything you want, Pirate Girl." He kissed the tip of her nose.

"I want the booty."

Epilogue

Embry hit the gas and the scooter flew forward. She screamed and grabbed the brake. "I'm scared."

Stede straddled the front tire of the scooter. "The first time I had you on my bike, I knew you were a natural born rider. You can do this. Once you get comfortable on the scooter, we'll move up to a real motorcycle."

"I know. Baby steps." She let out a breath. "Okay, move. I got this."

He squeezed her shoulders and stepped aside. She gave it some gas and took off slowly across the parking lot, picking her feet up and placing them on the footrest when she was going a little faster.

Stede had set up some cones to make a course so she could practice right and left turns, as well as straightaways and weaving.

When the wind hit her face, she relaxed her shoulders and let her mind wander.

The curator at the local Museum of Art had encouraged her to volunteer. It would look good on her resume when she applied for a job after graduation. She wasn't going to quit the sorority, but she was going to move out of the house at the end of the semester and in with Stede. The money she would save would help her afford to cut her hours at Pete's Place and put in some time at the museum.

They could move to D.C. after she graduated, and Stede could transfer to another school to finish his degree, but she'd decided she wasn't in a huge hurry to get out of South Carolina after all. She could get some practical work experience, and it gave them a few more years to be close to their families. Stede especially wanted more time after his overseas service.

Chase got kicked out of his fraternity and the college. He was being held in the county jail without bond until his court date. The rumor was he would get serious jail time since so many people filed charges against him.

Embry slowed to take a curve and picked up more speed on the straight stretch. A rush of adrenaline flooded her veins, and she knew she was where she was meant to be. She had the man she was meant to have. Her very own Gentleman Pirate.

He whistled and clapped when she approached and pulled to a stop.

Then he kissed her. "Way to go, Princess."

ABOUT THE AUTHOR

Meda White is an award-winning author who writes sweet, sultry, and southern contemporary and new adult romance. Born with Georgia clay running through her veins, she continues to enjoy the Southern lifestyle with her husband, a very spoiled Collie, and a stray cat who adopted the family. When not writing, you might find her making music, shooting zombie targets, teaching yoga, or explaining the meaning of her unusual first name.

A Note to Readers

Thank you for reading *Fall Rush*. It was interesting to explore some of the ways technology can get us into trouble. If you're interested in the other Southern College Novellas, stay tuned for a sneak peek at *Winter Formal.*

If you have a moment to leave an honest review, I'd really appreciate it. Not only do reviews let authors know how they're doing, they help readers find new books.

I love to hear from readers. Please look for me on my Website, Facebook, Twitter, and my Dirt Road Darlings street team. If you sign up for my Newsletter, which contains bonus material and sometimes prizes, it'll make sure you never miss a new release.

Thank you, and best wishes for a lifetime of love and laughter.

Meda

Winter Formal

Sibba Douglas opened the flap of her messenger bag and gasped. Her upper lip started sweating as she drew the bag closer to her body and away from Mike Ferguson, M.D. Maybe concealing the drug paraphernalia would make him unsee it.

"What's the matter?" Dr. Ferguson had a twinkle in his eye.

Sibba took a step back. "Nothing. It's just…I mean…I forgot my intern hours sheet. I'll bring it by next week so you can sign off for me."

Her sweaty hands slid on the strap of her bag. "Thanks again for letting me get my volunteer hours in your office, Doc. It's been a great experience."

"I'm glad you think so." The doctor turned to go and then paused. "I wonder if I can ask a favor?"

Her heart was in her throat. *Oh, God. If I say no, he'll rat me out.* "Yes, sir?"

"My godson is going to do his hours with me, if he can ever find the time. He's not doing very well in his sciences. I'm worried he won't be prepared for the MCAT in January."

Sibba swallowed, wondering what the favor was. Did he want her to take the test for his godson? Because she wouldn't do that. It was immoral. Unethical. Illegal. Like having a marijuana pipe in her messenger bag.

Oh, God. He might call the cops. Or worse, my dad. Her heart pummeled against her sternum.

"I was wondering if you could tutor him? His father and I grew up together in New York, so I've known him all his life. He's a good kid, just over-committed."

"Ah, yeah. Sure. I can do that." A bead of sweat ran from her hairline down to her jaw.

"Are you okay, Sibba?" He stepped toward her and put a hand on her arm.

She backed up. "Yes, sir. Fine. Just give him my number, and we'll set something up. Thanks again. See ya later."

She bolted for the back door. Once inside her rusting Mustang, which she'd cleverly named Rusty, she rested her forehead on the steering wheel and groaned.

Doc didn't say anything, but he had to have seen it. He was right beside her. How could anyone have missed the colorful blown glass pipe? It was possible he didn't know what it was for.

She beat her head against the wheel again.

Except, she was sure he did. He was a medical doctor. It was her goal to be a doctor someday, too. Preferably somewhere far away from the Southeastern U.S.; she wanted to see the world.

She wouldn't achieve her goals if she got caught with bud. She'd already promised herself she'd quit as soon as she got her acceptance letter from medical school. The urge to adjust the timetable was strong. But, the urge to burn one was stronger.

It would have to wait until she got home, as she wasn't in the habit of carrying it around. The pipe was a gift from her friend, Jon-Jon. He stopped by her place about once a week to check in, catch up, and annoy her roommate, Finlee. She should just give her stash to her roomie and be done with it.

A knock at her window made her jump and scream. Seeing it was the nurse, she rolled down her window.

"I'm taking the lab coats home to wash and noticed you forgot to leave yours."

Sibba looked down at the white coat she still wore. "Oh gosh, I'm sorry." She got out of the car and removed the jacket.

The nurse took it. "Don't hold your breath for that boy to call."

Sibba furrowed her brow. "What boy?"

"The godson."

She'd already forgotten. Her brain was fried. What started in high school as a way to have a little fun had become a habit. She was getting off the herb…for good.

ALSO BY MEDA WHITE

Spring Fling

A Southern College Novella

Kellyn Crenshaw wants to make it to college graduation without becoming another notch on the belt of a fraternity boy. A boy exactly like Pace Samson. Forced into close proximity because their roommates are dating, Kellyn sets out to prove she's resistant to his charms.

Pace never figured himself for a one-woman man until he spends time with Kellyn. She's different, and he can't get her out of his mind. She's also aware of his reputation, and it may keep him from the one girl who makes him want to change his ways.

When Pace and Kellyn fake a fling on Spring Break to help their friends, Kellyn may discover she isn't immune to Pace after all. They'll each have to decide if what's between them is just a fling or if there's a chance their feelings are real.

Winter Formal
A Southern College Novella

Life is going according to plan for Sibba Douglas until she gets blackmailed. Her future dream of being a doctor is threatened unless she can help a spoiled fraternity boy do well on the MCAT.

Nash Lincoln knows he needs to settle down and focus on his studies, but academics have taken a back seat to social events and he's coasting by on little sleep and lots of pills. The distraction of a tutor he's admired from afar isn't helping matters.

Substance abuse leads to tragedy and draws Sibba and Nash closer together. But it may also be the thing that tears them apart.

Christmas Give
A Holiday Novella

Eva Walker returns home to Georgia for the first Christmas since her husband's death. She's missed her family, but is afraid the void left by her husband will make it unbearable.

Between losing his job as an NFL defensive back and losing his wife to the star quarterback, Adam "Mack" Riggs has had a rough year. Looking for a change of pace, he visits an old college friend for Christmas.

The attraction between Eva and Adam is instant, and so is the laughter. Enjoying life again feels so good for both of them. Simple Christmas wishes unite with a shared holiday tradition, putting them on a path toward healing and acceptance. A path that could lead to a future, if only their pasts would remain where they belong.

Play With My Heart

A Southland Romance

Southern musician and closet geek Liz Baker enjoys her quiet life. While in Los Angeles helping her brother with a house project, the simple life gets complicated when British television actor Ian Clarke walks into the picture.

Ian enjoys his celebrity status in Hollywood and is determined nothing and no one will get in the way of his plans for success on the big screen. He never counted on meeting a woman like Liz, but she's the only one who can help him with a personal problem.

Forced into close quarters where priorities and cultures clash, an intense attraction catches them both by surprise. Secrets, old lovers and the paparazzi threaten their new dreams and a chance for love could be lost forever.

***Play With My Heart* is the 2014 BTS Red Carpet Award Winner in Contemporary Romance**.

Dance With My Heart: A Southland Romance Book 2
Ride With My Heart: A Southland Romance Book 3
Fool With My Heart: A Southland Romance Book 4